"You're still shaking," Levi said.

"I'm freezing." Kayla nodded. It was more than just the weather, but she could use something to take off the chill.

"Wait here." Levi doubled back and a minute later, he handed her a cup of hot chocolate. She took a sip, burning the tip of her tongue in the process.

"What are you thinking?" he asked as they headed toward the tram.

"I'm worried about what we're supposed to do if we end up finding Mercy. Even if we find her, we can't exchange her."

She turned to face him, tears pooling in her eyes. She needed to stay strong. Needed to keep her head clear, but all she could see was Mercy and her father lying on that slab in the morgue if they didn't stop these men. And they couldn't let that happen.

"Hey." He tilted up her chin with his hand until she was looking at him. "We're going to figure this out. I promise."

"And if we don't?"

He shook his head. "We have to. There's too much at stake."

Lisa Harris is a Christy Award winner and winner of the Best Inspirational Suspense Novel for 2011 from *RT Book Reviews*. She and her family are missionaries in southern Africa. When she's not working, she loves hanging out with her family, cooking different ethnic dishes, photography and heading into the African bush on safari. For more information about her books and life in Africa, visit her website at lisaharriswrites.com.

Books by Lisa Harris

Love Inspired Suspense

Final Deposit
Stolen Identity
Deadly Safari
Taken
Desperate Escape
Desert Secrets
Fatal Cover-Up
Deadly Exchange

DEADLY EXCHANGE

LISA HARRIS

HARLEQUIN® LOVE INSPIRED® SUSPENSE

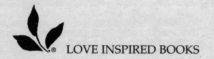

LOVE INSPIRED BOOKS

ISBN-13: 978-1-335-54352-3

Deadly Exchange

www.Harlequin.com

Printed in U.S.A.

For if thou altogether holdest thy peace at this time, then shall there enlargement and deliverance arise to the Jews from another place; but thou and thy father's house shall be destroyed: and who knoweth whether thou art come to the kingdom for such a time as this?
—Esther 4:14

To the men and women across the globe whose fight for justice is changing lives, one at a time.

ONE

Kayla Brooks balanced one foot on the bike pedal and the other on the reddish path then waited for the traffic light to turn green. Getting around a city like Amsterdam, where there were more bikes than people, had initially felt like traversing a minefield. But after living here for two years, the choice to navigate the city like the locals was a no-brainer. Not only was it cheaper than public transportation, it was also faster.

A scooter zipped past her down the winding street as the light turned green. Ignoring her irritation, she started through the intersection—supposedly reserved for bicycles—and picked up her pace while mentally going through her to-do list. With the upcoming annual fund-raising luncheon only two weeks away, her list had grown substantially. Which meant she'd have to postpone running the bulk of her personal errands—like restocking her empty fridge—at least until the weekend.

The squeal of brakes jerked her out of her thoughts.

Kayla glanced behind her just in time to see a car swerve toward her. It slammed into her back tire, throwing her onto the hard pavement face-first. A sharp pain shot through her elbow as she started to untangle herself from her bike. The car flew past, its driver never looking back.

A shot of adrenaline raced through her as she glanced back at the string of bikes coming toward her. She needed to get off the path before she got run over. A man in a business suit riding a sturdy bike swerved out of the way, just barely avoiding hitting her. He shouted a few choice words as he flew past, chastising her both for being a tourist and for blocking the path.

So much for trying to blend in and look like a local.

Five seconds later, she managed to drag her bike out of the line of traffic to a strip of grass, barely avoiding another near collision with a woman riding with her toddler. She examined the damage—first on her body. Besides skinned-up palms and the lingering pain in her arm, nothing seemed broken. As for the bike she'd affectionately named Archie, the back fender was bent and the tire wouldn't move.

Great. There was no way the damaged heap of metal was going to get her home.

She looked back down the street where the offending car had disappeared and let out a sharp huff of frustration. A couple people zoomed by on their bikes, apparently not having seen what had just happened. Her options were limited. She was going to have to lock up her bike, then walk the rest of the way home. She'd deal with the messed-up tire later.

Her phone buzzed as she snapped the padlock into place, securing her bike to a post. She glanced at the string of text messages.

do i have your attention now?

go home and wait for us to contact you again.

and don't go to the police or there will be consequences.

Consequences?
A sick feeling spread through her. What kind of consequences?
Her stomach heaved. She stood on the side

of the road, trying to interpret the messages. They had to be connected to her work. It was the only thing that made sense. She'd known when she accepted a position with International Freedom Operation that helping women who'd been trafficked get off the streets was risky. Three months ago, one of the girls they'd tried to rescue had been murdered, bringing with it a string of unwanted memories of her own. The girl's death had been a frightening reminder of exactly whom they were dealing with on a day-to-day basis. And while threats weren't uncommon, what did they—whoever *they* were—want from her?

Deciding to take a risk, she quickly punched in a number on her phone and then waited for her coworker to answer as she started walking.

"Evi? This is Kayla."

"Kayla…where are you? You sound out of breath."

"I'm walking home—"

"Walking? What happened to your bike?"

"It's out of commission." Kayla glanced behind her at the traffic zooming past her, trying not to give in to the panic. "Someone just hit me, and it wasn't…it wasn't an accident."

"Wait a minute. A hit-and-run? Did you call the police—"

"No… I can't."

"What do you mean you can't?"

"I'm probably not supposed to be talking to you, but I don't know what else to do. I also got a couple of text messages. I don't know who they're from, but they told me not to go to the police. I think it might be connected with one of the girls we're working with."

"Kayla, if that's true, I don't care what they told you. If someone's threatening you, we need to get the authorities involved. Take the tram to the office, and we'll meet you there as soon as we can."

"I'm almost home," Kayla said. "I think I'd rather be there, since it will be dark soon. Plus I need to check on my father and make sure he's okay."

She started walking faster. She'd be safe in her apartment, and it would give her a place to think. At least she thought she'd be safe. She tried to shake off the torrent of fearful thoughts.

I have no idea how to deal with this, God. The decision to work with IFO came with its own set of risks, but this—having my life threatened…

What was she supposed to do?

"Okay, listen," Evi said. "Abel and I can try to catch the next train out of Maastricht, but it will still be several hours until we can get back to Amsterdam. In the meantime, go home and stay there until we get back and the three of us can figure out what to do. I don't think the girls need to know what's happening yet, but I'll contact each of them and make sure they're okay."

Kayla hung up the call a minute later. They'd done everything they could to cover all the bases with the trafficked girls they were helping reintegrate into society and regain their independence as they healed emotionally. They'd also put into place a detailed emergency protocol. Until they knew what they were looking at, she couldn't have any of the girls' lives put at risk.

She glanced again at her phone. But what did these people want?

Another message came through with another photo.

I thought we were clear. Talk to no one. No police. No one at your work.

She clicked on the photo and saw a picture of herself sprawled on the bicycle path.

They were watching.

Ten minutes later, Kayla stepped into her apartment and slid the security bolt shut behind her. The panic that had started when the car had hit her only managed to grow as she double-checked the lock. She needed some kind of weapon. She glanced around the tiny entryway, then grabbed the broom before starting through the two-bedroom apartment to make sure no one was inside.

She flipped on the overhead light and felt her breath catch. Someone had been here. The files that had been on her desk now lay scattered across the floor, and her laptop was open to the password prompt. Thieves would have taken the computer. Whoever had broken in had been looking for something. But what?

"Dad? Dad, are you here?"

Her heartbeat quickened as she checked the room where her father, Max, had been staying the past few weeks. A pile of books that had been on his bedside table lay strewn across the floor next to his radio. Had he been out when someone had broken in, or had they walked in on him? She couldn't tell, but one thing was clear—he wasn't here now.

She tried to squelch the growing panic. Chances were he'd simply run down to the corner café for an early dinner. Or at least that's what she hoped had happened. But it was going to be dark soon, and he never stayed out after dark…

She grabbed her phone out of her back pocket and dialed his number.

No answer.

She hung up the call, trying to convince herself that everything was still somehow okay. That her father not answering didn't mean something had happened to him. How many times over the past few weeks had she reminded him to keep his phone on so she could contact him if she needed him? For all she knew, he'd left the phone somewhere here in the house.

Still, worry began to spread. She'd invited her father to stay with her for a couple months, praying that a change of pace would help with the pain of losing her mom eight months ago to acute kidney failure. With the loss had come the familiar signs of depression he'd experienced before, but so far, she wasn't sure the change of pace was helping. Until recently, he'd rarely left the apartment, spending most of his time in the small room she'd fixed up for him, listening to the news on his radio or reading.

Something creaked above her. She glanced up. It was probably just her neighbors upstairs. She quickly finished checking her bedroom and her bathroom, then peeked out onto the small balcony that was just big enough to store her bike and found the intruder's point of entry. Someone had wedged open the balcony window. But whoever had broken in was gone.

Her phone rang, bringing on another flood of adrenaline. She set down the broom, then glanced at the caller ID, disappointed when it wasn't her father. Surely they couldn't monitor her movements from inside her own apartment.

"Hello?"

"Kayla?"

"Who is this?"

"It's Levi Cummings. Listen, I know it's been a long time," he rushed on, "but I really need to talk to you. It's…it's about Adam. He's in Amsterdam."

Her head began to throb at the news. How was that possible? Adam was supposed to be in prison.

She contemplated hanging up. Instead, she melted into the leather chair in the corner of her bedroom, wondering what else life was going to throw at her today. Almost two years had passed since she'd walked out of that busy courtroom. One year and eleven months, give or take a day or two. Not that she was counting. Because she wasn't. But it had been enough time to send back all of the wedding and shower gifts, as well as inform the guests that there was not going to be a ceremony. Instead, she'd donated her white satin dress to charity and started a new life, determined to recover from a broken engagement.

She hadn't told people why the wedding had been canceled. She hadn't had to. Adam Cummings's arrest had been all over the news at the time: Groom Arrested for Fraud. Bride Left at the Altar.

Not literally at the altar, but it had been close enough. Three weeks after his sentence, she'd decided to accept a position with International Freedom Operation that would expand the nonprofit she worked for into Europe. She'd taken the next flight to Amsterdam, hoping to put her past—and all the bad memories—behind her.

"Kayla, are you still there?"

"Yes, I'm here. Sorry. It's just that…hearing from you caught me off guard."

She stood up and started pacing the small bedroom. She had enough on her plate today. Talking with her ex-fiancé's brother really wasn't something she had the emotional energy to deal with at the moment. Her elbow ached from the fall, and she needed to take some pain medicine. Except even pain medicine wasn't going to be able to mask reality.

"Levi... I'm sorry." She ran her finger across a row of books. "I don't understand why Adam would be here. I thought he was still in prison."

"He got out early for good behavior, and I have reason to believe that he's in Amsterdam to see you."

She frowned. She had no desire to see Adam, though she hadn't exactly kept up with the news. The last time her mother had sent her an article from back home it had been about Arkansas' most eligible bachelor, Levi Cummings, who according to the magazine was also quite a ladies' man. The up-and-coming CEO of Potterville was also known as the man who'd saved the small town from dying out.

She shifted her mind back to the conversation.

"How long has he been out?"

"Five days."

"Why would he want to see me? We didn't exactly part on good terms." Unless...unless he was the one behind what was happening today.

"Honestly, I'm not sure he would come, but that's why I'm worried."

Worried that your little brother is about to cause another scandal?

She squeezed her eyes shut for a few seconds and tried to steady her breath. "I'm still not following you."

There was a long pause on the line. "You heard some of the things he said about you when he left for prison. Threats he made."

"Like blaming me for his arrest?"

She stared at a stain on the carpet that needed to be cleaned. The hit-and-run, the cryptic text messages... Was all of this because Adam still blamed her for his arrest? Something wasn't adding up. She knew Adam—or at least she once had. And while she might not have any desire to see him again, she'd never believe he'd try to hurt her.

Or would he?

He'd spent the past two years in prison. Enough time to think about the person he blamed for putting him there and come up with a plan for revenge.

"Kayla?"

"I just can't believe he'd do anything to hurt me," she said.

"I'll be honest, I haven't seen him much these past couple of years. His choice. But he believes—or at least at one time believed—

that if you hadn't gone to the police, then he wouldn't have gotten arrested."

"For one," she began, "it was the authorities who came to me. And on top of that, at the time I had no idea what Adam was involved in. But that part of my life is over, and I have no intentions of going back."

"Please, I'm not trying to upset you, but I do want to make sure you're safe. Which is why I think it would be better if we spoke in person."

"Wait a minute. You're in Amsterdam as well?"

"I just arrived in the city. I thought we could discuss what's going on, and how we're going to resolve the situation."

She let out an audible sigh. Spoken like a true army intelligence officer. Like he was on a combat operation and needed information in order to protect her. But maybe she shouldn't be surprised. Levi had always been incredibly focused. Which was why, even though he and Adam were only eleven months apart, Levi had always played the role of older brother. Even to the point that when his father had gotten sick, he'd been the one to complete his current contract with the military and then returned to rural Arkansas to run his family's manufacturing company. And as always, he'd continued to be the glue that held the Cummings family together during a crisis.

Like when his father had come to her, insulting her by offering fifty thousand dollars not to tell her side of the story. The whole situation had made her question—not for the first time—her whirlwind relationship with Adam that had made her miss noticing that there was nothing solid beneath his charm. It made her realize as well that she'd simply been enamored to the point where she wasn't sure if she'd ever really loved him. Because it hadn't been Adam who'd come to her rescue. In the end, Levi had been the one who'd stood up for her, sweeping in and cleaning up the mess.

But none of that mattered. Not anymore.

Kayla pressed her fingers against her temples. Her decision to come to Amsterdam and her rejection of that money had nothing to do with what was happening today. She'd always known she'd made the right decision, not letting the Cummings family buy her out. Not that she ever would have divulged what she knew about them.

"Kayla, please...has Adam contacted you?"

"No."

"Then we need to meet before he does."

Kayla frowned. Apparently this problem wasn't going away, either.

"Where are you?" she asked.

"Near the city center, but I can come to you."

"I live a bit farther out."

"That's fine. If you give me the address, I've already secured a taxi."

Of course he had. He had flown across the Atlantic, hired a taxi and was now prepared to fix things. Just like he always did.

But the last thing she wanted to do was get involved in Adam's life—or with anyone from the Cummings family, for that matter. Maybe the sooner she saw Levi, the sooner she could put all of this behind her.

"Fine." She gave him her address, thought about suggesting they discuss whatever it was they needed to discuss over dinner, then decided that would be far too personal. He could come, say whatever it was he needed to say, then leave.

"Are you sure you're okay?" he asked.

"I'm fine. It's just…it's been a rough day." She hesitated before continuing. She didn't want to believe Adam was capable of hurting her, but Levi was right. Adam had threatened her, blaming her for his arrest. "I'll explain when you get here."

"Then I'll be there in about thirty minutes," he said.

She hung up the phone, then downed a couple of aspirin with a glass of cold water. She needed to figure out if it was Adam who was targeting her—or someone far more deadly.

Levi Cummings stood outside Kayla's apartment, trying to get his nerve up to knock on the door. Which was ridiculous. He'd spent the past two years running a multimillion-dollar manufacturing compound and employing thousands of workers, which had in turn lowered the town's unemployment to just over 4 percent. All thanks to the Cummings family. Or so their head of PR always liked to say. But while he missed his work in the army, family had always been a priority. He'd decided to put his whole heart into building a company that provided jobs by creating the tents and outdoor gear that had become income for their town.

In the process, though, financial meetings and other responsibilities had filled up his calendar, making it so he couldn't even remember the last time he'd actually had a chance to head out with any of his company's gear for a day of hiking and fishing. But he knew how to handle conflict. So how had it come to the place where he was scared to knock on the door of an old friend? It was just Kayla Brooks. The girl next door. The girl he'd known forever. The girl who'd stolen his heart in seventh grade and who'd now somehow managed to bring him across the Atlantic just to ensure she was okay. What he hadn't been able to do—at least not completely—was convince himself that he wasn't responding out of emotion or any personal reasons. Was his being here simply a matter of family honor?

He knocked on the door, rolled back on his heels, then stuffed his hands into his pockets while he waited for her to answer. She finally did, a full thirty seconds later.

"Levi." Her gaze took him in. "It's been a long time."

"Almost two years. How are you?"

She hadn't changed. Not really. She still had the same wide hazel eyes, red hair that now reached past her shoulders and a sprinkle of freckles across her cheeks. She looked... beautiful. Not that it mattered.

"I'm fine. Just wondering why you flew all the way to Europe to see me. And why Adam would want to see me."

She'd made her feelings clear the last time they'd spoken, on the day of Adam's sentence. Levi had walked her out to the car, begging her not to take offense at how his father had tried to buy her off. Ira Cummings was used to getting what he wanted, and used to using money as a bargaining chip to get it—whether it was someone's cooperation or someone's silence. And this time the seventy-year-old patriarch had wanted to ensure that Kayla wouldn't do anything that might further ruin the Cummings family name.

But his father should have known her better than that. Levi could have told him before he handed her the check that Kayla wasn't the kind of person to take a bribe. She wouldn't tell her story to the paper, or anyone else for that matter, because she was one of the few people he knew who still actually held to their principles. He'd always found that refreshing. It was his father who hadn't seen it that way.

Kayla, though, had always been different, and she'd never do anything to hurt those around her or the town she'd grown up in. With a population of just under seven thousand, the town boasted a turn-of-the-century courthouse, a white water tower painted with the local high school mascot and Reggie's diner, known in a hundred-mile-radius for the best catfish, fried okra and apple fritters.

Levi knew Kayla loved that town as much as he did.

She stepped back from the doorway. "You can come in."

He nodded, wondering how he was supposed to greet her. A hug seemed too personal at the moment, so he just thanked her, then stepped inside the cozy living room with its hardwood floors. The apartment was small, but the living room had a large window that would ensure plenty of light in the adjoining dining area and tiny galley kitchen during the day. She'd added a few personal touches, mainly some artwork on the walls, photos of friends and family that were stuck on the refrigerator and a vase full of purple and white tulips on the table, a surprise for February. What also surprised him was that it wasn't neat and organized like he expected. As if someone had hurriedly gone through her things.

Levi frowned. Whatever was going on, she was clearly upset about something. "When's the last time you heard from Adam?" he asked, getting straight to the point of his visit.

"I haven't. I made it clear two years ago that things were over between us. I don't know why he'd want to see me now."

"Neither do I, but that's why I'm here."

"Trying to avoid another family scandal?"

He brushed off the biting comment. "I'm not my father."

"No, but surely you haven't forgotten the fifty thousand dollars he tried to give me, or the choice words and the long lecture it came with."

"I haven't forgotten, but I didn't come to threaten you, Kayla. I came here to warn you."

"About Adam?" She sat down on the couch and offered him a worn wing chair across from her. "He might have made some bad choices, but he wouldn't hurt me."

"Are you sure about that?"

"I'm pretty sure that Adam is the least of my worries right now."

"What do you mean?"

She glanced at her phone lying on the table as if she were trying to decide what to tell him. "It's nothing. Just some things I need to take care of. You didn't need to come, Levi."

"I'm not so sure about that."

"Then how long do you plan to stay in the country?"

He studied her body language. She seemed on edge…distracted. Something was off. "Until I'm sure you're safe."

"I'm fine."

"You don't seem fine." He leaned forward. He might be pressing for something that wasn't any of his business, but he could tell by her eyes that something was wrong. "Because you clearly seem scared about something, and if you're convinced Adam would never hurt you, then it's about something else."

She mindlessly grabbed a piece of candy from a bowl on the table between them, tugged off the wrapper, then popped the sweet into her mouth.

"Where's your dad?" he asked, his concern rising. "I heard he was staying with you."

"He is, but…to be honest, I'm not sure where he is."

Levi leaned forward, waiting for her to continue.

"I received some other messages today. Some…threats. But I'm pretty sure they weren't from Adam."

"Can I see them?"

She hesitated before picking up her phone. "You don't have to come to my rescue. I'm not ten anymore."

A memory surfaced. The three of them had decided to take a shortcut home from school. Adam had tried to convince them no one would ever know they'd trespassed, but Mr. Sander's bull had had other ideas. Levi had managed to pull Kayla over the fence to safety, even though she'd quickly assured him after the rescue that she could have scaled the fence on her own.

She'd always been stubborn, even though he'd joked in return that she owed him for saving her life.

"And this photo?" he asked. "You could have been seriously hurt."

"But I wasn't." She shook her head. "And while I could be wrong, I don't think these texts are from your brother, Levi. They just don't sound like him."

He read through the messages again. "I wouldn't have flown all the way here if I didn't think Adam was capable of following through with his threats."

"Maybe, but there's another possibility."

He looked up and caught her gaze. "What do you mean?"

"I think the threats could be related to my work."

"I know some about the nonprofit you work for, but how?"

"We work with exploited and trafficked women, and not everyone is happy about what we do."

"Have you received threats before?"

"Not personally, but others involved with

the work have. We're combating a hundred-billion-dollar business. We get girls off the streets, which means while there might be someone else to take the place of the girls we rescue, someone's losing their income."

She was scared. He could see it in her body language and in her eyes.

"What about the police?" he asked. "Have you told them what's going on?"

"Not yet. I'm not sure they can help. Traffickers use burner phones and know how to work under the radar."

"Maybe, but you still don't know who's behind this. And even if it is traffickers, the police have got to have resources that will help, or has legalizing prostitution changed things?"

"It shifted the role of pimps and traffickers to businessmen and managers. And while some do choose this life, there are still many who are being imported into this country in order to meet the demand—including children. They are promised work but end up trapped in a world they can't get out of."

"And in the meantime, the traffickers are making money," he said. "I'm just not sure you should shrug this off. You could have been killed when that car hit your bike."

"But I wasn't."

"No, but this clearly isn't over."

Kayla's phone beeped, and she picked it up.

He studied her face, trying to ignore the unexpected feelings he still held for her. Because falling for his brother's ex-fiancée would not be a good move. He'd tried to tell himself that he was only here because he felt sorry for her. She was simply an old friend, and he didn't want anything to happen to her. But it was personal, and he wanted to help her. If he had his way, he'd take her back to the US on the next flight if he could confirm her life was in danger.

A second later her face paled.

"What's wrong, Kayla?"

She stared at the phone. "They've got my father."

"What?"

"They sent a video."

"Who?"

"I don't know."

Her hand shook as she passed him the phone. He watched the ten-second video of Max sitting in a chair with his hands tied behind him as he spoke.

"Kayla... I'm so sorry. They're demanding that you hand over one of your girls—Mercy—in the next twenty-four hours. Or they've said they will kill me."

TWO

The street below blurred as Kayla stared out her apartment window. Car headlights streaked by, houseboats moored on the canal bobbed in the water and the endless rows of houses were lit up by hazy streetlamps and porch lights. Her mind tried to work through the logic of what she'd just seen on the video. How in the world had this happened? Someone had entered her apartment, snatched her father and was now threatening to kill him?

"Why take my father?" she asked, speaking her thoughts out loud to Levi. "He has nothing to do with my work."

"They need leverage. They're using him to get to you."

So those were the consequences they'd meant. If she didn't find Mercy, they'd kill her father.

How did a job helping people come to this? She studied the pedestrians and bikes passing below. Were they out there, watching her apartment? It seemed impossible to tell in the darkness. No one looked out of place, but that didn't mean they weren't there. A chill blew through her, raising goose bumps across her forearm.

If they were out there now...watching her...

Maybe she was just being paranoid. They'd given her twenty-four hours to find Mercy, which meant for the next twenty-four hours it was to their advantage to keep her father alive. Because right now, he was the only leverage they had.

And when she found Mercy? What was she supposed to do then?

Levi crossed the room, stopping beside her. "Tell me about Mercy. Who is she?"

"One of the girls we've been working with the past few months. About eighteen months ago, she was brought to Italy from Nigeria with promises of a job and money to send back to her parents. Once she got there, she found out that everything she'd been told was a bunch of lies."

"And now her previous...owner...wants her back?"

Kayla nodded. It was an impossible trade. An impossible situation with no easy resolution. Trade Mercy for Max, or let her father die. How was she supposed to do either one?

There has to be another way, God.

"She's only seventeen years old, Levi."

"I don't think this is something you can fix on your own, Kayla." He stepped up next to her. "You need to go to the police. It's the only way out of this."

"They told me not to go to the police." She was trying not to panic, but while she'd always known there were risks to her job, everything had suddenly spiraled out of control. And now her choices were causing consequences in other people's lives. People she loved. "I can't risk them hurting my father."

"And do you think that *not* going to the police is going to help?" Levi asked. "At least we'd have more resources on our side."

"We?" She took a step back, immediately regretting the sharp tone of her voice. "I'm sorry, but you don't need to get involved in this. Two of my coworkers, Evi and Abel, are on their way back to Amsterdam right now. We will figure out something."

"I thought they told you not to get your coworkers involved. Besides, the moment I got on that plane to Europe, I was involved. And whether your life's at risk because of my brother or a bunch of human traffickers doesn't really matter at this point. There's no way I can just walk away."

"What about Adam?" she said. "Do you know where he is?"

"I haven't been able to get a hold of him."

She glanced up at him, suddenly grateful to have a familiar face next to her right now. This was the Levi she remembered. The man she'd always known him to be. Fiercely loyal, he would never walk away from ensuring the good guys won. It was what had propelled him to join the military in order to serve his country, as well as what had motivated him to return home when his family needed him.

But still. How could she expect him to help fight her battle?

"I need to see if I can get a hold of Mercy. Then I need to come up with a plan to get my father back as well, because…because I don't know what else to do." She pressed her lips together. She was rambling. A habit she had when she was nervous. She grabbed her phone off the table then caught his gaze. "And, Levi…thank you."

"You're welcome. I'm just glad I'm here."

Kayla dialed Mercy's number, praying she picked up. The phone went straight to voice mail.

"Her phone's off."

"Tell me more about the connection to your job. I know you work with International Freedom Operation, but all I know is what's on their website."

"Many of the girls we help, like Mercy, lived in extreme poverty before making the journey here. When they learn of travel brokers offering visas and a plane ticket to Europe, they believe they've found a way to support their family."

"And yet it's all a lie," Levi said.

Kayla nodded. "They're now indebted to the people who smuggled them into the country and forced to work in the sex trade. We help those who have been able to escape with a place to live, job training, language classes and sometimes even citizenship."

"So this is probably about someone who believes you're getting in the way of what they're doing?"

She nodded. "I know what they can do, Levi. They won't hesitate to kill my father if I don't do what they say. Or kill me if they don't get what they want. Three months ago, one of our girls was found dead. The authorities concluded it was an overdose, but I never believed that. She'd been clean, happy and was doing well in our program. I talked to her the day before she went missing. She was excited about her future. I'll never believe she simply went back willingly to the men who'd trafficked her."

Levi caught her gaze and held it. "Like your sister, Lilly?"

Kayla took a sharp intake of breath at the mention of her sister.

"I'm sorry, I just know how personal this must be—"

"No," she said. "It's fine. I just… I miss Lilly so much. Next week is the seventh anniversary of the day we found her. Sometimes it still seems unreal. And Mercy…she reminds me so much of my sister. Funny, outgoing…"

Her mind shifted momentarily to the day the FBI came to their door to tell them they'd found Lilly's body. The moment that had erased any hope they'd find her alive.

"I only know what my mother forwarded to me via the local news," Levi said, "but it was enough for me to know how painful it had to have been for you. And in turn how personal all of this is. I sent you a letter after Lilly's funeral. I don't know if you ever got it, but I just wanted you to know I was thinking about you. Praying for your family. I know I can't begin to imagine what you all were going through."

She sat back down in the living room chair,

her thoughts switching to the pile of envelopes that had slowly stacked up after her sister's disappearance. There had been hundreds of cards from friends and family. "I do remember. Yours was one of the few handwritten letters. I hope you didn't take it personally if we didn't respond. There were so many cards and messages. First around the time of her disappearance, then a few months later at her funeral. I was just trying to keep my family together."

"I didn't mention the letter to make you feel guilty. I just wanted you to know that I had been thinking about you and your family."

"I know." She waved her hand in front of her, wishing it was just as easy to wave away the accumulated years of grief. "It wasn't supposed to happen to Lilly. Not to a middle-class girl living in a small town where violent crime was rarer than a blizzard in July. It changed the fabric of my family. And of the entire town, really. It's like the bubble we'd been living in burst, and people realized suddenly that what happened to Lilly could happen to anyone."

Her eyes filled with tears. Even with all the time that had passed, she still hadn't healed. Not completely. And she wasn't sure she ever would.

* * *

Levi leaned forward to brush a strand of hair off her shoulder, then pulled back at the too-intimate gesture. He'd come to ensure she stayed safe. Nothing more.

"The scary thing is that it really can happen to anyone anywhere." Her lashes were wet when she looked up at him. "These girls… they never expected to have to deal with what they have had to live through. And now…they have my father."

As much as he didn't want to pull her away from her grief, he needed to get her back on track. Her father's life was at stake. And his might not be the only one.

"You mentioned an emergency plan. What exactly is Mercy supposed to do if she believes her life is in danger?"

"While we always hope we never have to use it, each girl has an emergency protocol in case their trafficker—or someone else—comes after them. We teach them what to do if they're followed, how to get out of their apartment safely, who to call using code words if they are under duress and access to a safe house we have set up."

"Tell me more about the safe house."

"If any of the girls feel as if their lives are in danger, they are to call it in, then go directly to the safe house. The procedure was implemented because most of the girls—because of where they come from—are afraid of the authorities and don't want to deal with them. It's near public transportation so it's easy to get to, and once there, they are given a cell phone to text me with the code that tells me where they are and that they are safe."

"But Mercy hasn't done any of these things."

Kayla shook her head. "No. Which has me worried. I know Mercy. Maybe she doesn't know they're after her, but I found out right before you got here that she didn't show up for work or her class tonight."

"So you think she ran?"

"If they had her, they wouldn't need me. So something had to have spooked her. Made her believe she was better off on her own than going to the safe house."

"Have you ever used the system before?"

"The girl I told you about earlier, the one who was killed, she was being stalked by her former pimp. The last thing I got from her was her distress message."

"Which might give Mercy motivation to do things on her own. Where do you think she would go?"

"I don't know." Kayla closed the living

room curtains, turned on a lamp next to the couch, then sat down. "Most of the girls don't have a lot of friends other than each other. They're working hard for a better life and don't have a lot of free time."

Levi took the chair across from her. "Then help me understand what she's thinking right now."

Kayla let out a slow breath while her fingers played with the hem of her shirt. "By the time they get to us, they are suffering from PTSD. Most of them have been beaten over and over. Some of them have even been branded. They've been cut off from everyone. They are afraid to go to the authorities and too ashamed to go to friends or family. Coming to us—and working through our program—takes a tremendous amount of courage."

He could hear the passion in her voice as she spoke about the girls she worked with. Her compassion for these women paired with her strong desire for justice had created a huge part of the motivation for her to do what she did. And on top of that—with the loss of her sister—the motivation behind what she did was personal.

"So how does someone like Mercy find you?" he asked.

"Getting out is often the hardest part. On one hand, they're terrified of physical retribution if they leave. They're also trapped mentally, so even if they could escape, many of them don't because they are already isolated from friends and family. Girls like Mercy, who are from other countries, don't have any identification papers and are terrified they'll get arrested for being illegal.

"In Mercy's situation, a Good Samaritan took her to the hospital after finding her beaten up in a hotel room. We work with other agencies, and often it's the first responders who come to us with the girls, which is how she was eventually brought to us. Unfortunately too many of these girls don't find a way out."

Kayla's phone buzzed again. She snatched it off the table.

"What is it this time?" Levi asked. If it was Mercy...

A second later she held up the phone so he could see it.

You didn't listen to me. I told you not to get anyone involved. If you want to keep your father safe, you will do what I say.

She clicked on the attached photo. It was one of her and Levi standing at the window.

"Kayla—"

"They're watching," she said, quickly crossing the room to pull back the curtain and peer down again on the darkened street.

"You're not going to find them," he said, joining her at the window.

"I know."

Levi felt his anger simmer as he followed her gaze to the cafés and shops, rows of bikes and pedestrians walking by. But someone was out there. Watching Kayla like they had been when she was on the street. Watching her again while she stood in the privacy of her home. His concern for Max and Mercy hadn't changed, but now he was worried about her as well.

"If the message was meant to scare me, they've done exactly that," she said. "I'm terrified. What am I supposed to do?"

He drew in a deep breath, mentally going through their options. "I think you should play their game."

"Play their game? What do you mean?"

"I think you should respond."

"How?"

He knew it was taking a risk, but anything

they did at this point was risky. At least she wasn't doing this on her own.

"Can I see your phone?"

She handed it to him, and he started typing.

You want me to find Mercy? Let me do it my way. I'll find her faster if I have help.

He showed her the text.

"So we make him believe we'll actually make the trade?"

"For the moment, yes. And I think they'll believe you. Why wouldn't they? They already believe you'll choose your father over Mercy or they wouldn't have taken him for leverage."

He waited while she mulled over his suggestion.

"What if this makes them mad?" she asked.

"I'd say they're already mad. Making them think you're planning on following through with their plan is to your advantage."

"Okay. Send it."

He glanced back at the screen, praying his analysis of the situation was correct, and pressed Send. In the army he'd been trained to process strategic intelligence on the enemy. This was really no different. He needed to pull together all the information he could then come up with a battle plan.

He stared at the screen as if that was going to bring a quicker reply. "Do you have any idea who might be behind this?"

She shook her head as she headed toward her bedroom. "I've got copies of her file locked up in my safe. I don't remember any names mentioned in her files, but I do know that she was bought and sold several times. First in Italy. Then here in Holland."

"So we can't just automatically narrow it down."

She came back a minute later with a thin file folder. "I might be able to find something in here, but no one was arrested in connection to her situation. And any names we had were aliases."

"Which is going to make our job harder."

Another text came through. Kayla read the text then handed the phone to Levi.

Fine, but you better find her.

"What do you suggest we do?" She heard the impatience in her voice and pressed her lips together. She wasn't trying to be difficult. She just wanted to find a way to fix the situation without making things worse. And she had no idea how.

"Let's start with Mercy's apartment."

Kayla glanced out the window. "And if they try to follow us?"

"We have to make sure they don't."

THREE

Kayla dropped Mercy's file into her bag, then reached to take the keys to her apartment off the table. But the keys slipped through her fingers and onto the floor.

"Kayla?"

"Sorry." She held her trembling hands out in front of her, then balled her fingers into fists. "I'm trying not to panic. Trying not to imagine what they might do to my father. He's been through a lot this past year with my mother dying. Not to mention how hard he took my sister's death. I'm not sure how much more he's going to be able to endure."

Levi's fingers wrapped around hers, an unexpected steadying force in the middle of the storm. "I remember your father and always looked up to him as an honest leader in the community. I can only begin to imagine how hard this is on both of you, but he's a strong man, Kayla."

"I know, but now…"

Her words faded. How was either of them supposed to deal with this? Maybe she was underestimating her father, but she'd seen how much he'd lost and how he'd responded to that loss. She'd watched his fight against depression and the numbness that had seemed to consume him. He'd managed to hold on to his faith, but even that had become a day-to-day struggle. She'd hoped his coming to live with her would give him a new perspective, but it had only been recently that he'd started leaving the apartment. Going for walks in the morning, occasionally stopping at a pancake house for a stack of *pannekoeken* filled with spiced apples, syrup and whipped cream. But she knew that the healing over her mother's death had barely begun.

"I think you should give him some credit," Levi said, picking up her keys before pressing them gently against her palm. "He's lost a lot in his lifetime. First your sister, and now your mom. But that doesn't change the fact that he will pull through and find the strength he needs to get through this."

"We got in a fight this morning," she said. "It was over something stupid. I'd been bugging him to get out more. I thought I was trying to help him, but now…now I'd do anything just to know he was sitting safe on my couch."

"We'll find him. We'll find Mercy, and we'll figure out a way to save them both."

"But how? Even if we find Mercy, we can't trade her for my father. And yet if we don't trade her, they'll kill him." She looked up at Levi and caught his gaze, feeling the enormous pressure of needing answers. "I'm sorry I got you involved in this. Both you and my father."

"None of this is your fault. I came to make sure you were okay, and just because the threat has changed, my desire to keep you safe hasn't."

She wondered why it mattered to him. Why, after all these years, had he taken the time out of his busy schedule to keep her safe?

"Is the place close enough to walk?" Levi asked. "Or should we call for a taxi?"

"We can take the tram." She pulled on her coat and scarf, then paused in the doorway. "And if you want to come with me, I'd like that."

Kayla locked the door behind them before starting down the narrow staircase to the ground floor. Until she knew exactly who was behind this, it couldn't hurt to have a bodyguard. Levi's time in the military had given him an extra layer of strength and confidence. The same strength and confidence he'd ended up taking with him to the boardroom.

But even Levi's presence didn't completely settle her nerves as she stepped onto the busy street. Because the bottom line was that someone *was* threatening her. She studied the crowds as they headed out on foot. The narrow avenues around her house were always busy with cars, bicycles and scooters, along with a constant flow of pedestrians. She hurried beside him along the canal, with its tall, skinny row houses that all seemed to lean slightly askew reflecting in the water.

Someone clanged the bell on their handlebars. She jumped out of the way, her heart pounding as the bike zoomed past. Pressing her hand against her chest, she took in a deep breath, trying to slow her breathing. She was going to have to find a way to calm her panic.

"You actually ride your bike out here?" Levi asked.

"You get used to it. Most of the time. And besides, it's the easiest way to get around."

"Maybe, but when I go riding or hiking, I prefer not to be in the middle of the city."

"There's more to explore than just the city, even though the country's flat terrain is not quite as rugged or even as beautiful as Arkansas." She jumped into the trivial conversation, needing a distraction from the video of her father that continued to replay in her mind. "Last month, a couple friends and I headed out of the city on a twenty-mile route past a castle known as Muiderslot, then followed one of the scenic canals into the countryside."

"Now that sounds like a challenge I'd enjoy."

"You should try it one day."

She glanced at him, hoping he didn't think she'd meant it as an invitation for him to spend time with her. But she knew that Levi had never steered away from a challenge, whether it was hiking the Ouachita Trail, rock climbing on Mount Magazine or running a marathon.

Today, it seemed, keeping her safe was his challenge.

She grew silent again as they walked. The narrow canal and its bridges reminded her of Paris, though that was where the similarity ended. The architecture of the city was unique, with its tall, narrow buildings, their rows of windows all reflecting the water. He seemed content to let her set the pace as they continued past a row of merchants, who during the day sold flowers and bulbs from floating barges.

"It's closed now, but this is one of my favorite places to walk through, though I confess I don't have a green thumb. At all," she said, breaking the silence between them for another inconsequential discussion. "I bought some tulip bulbs once and thought I'd grow some out on my balcony. A year later, there's still just a pile of dirt in the flower box."

"That's a shame, because I saw photos of this place on the plane, and the flowers were stunning," he said.

"They are. This flower market has been floating on the Singel canal since the mid-1800s. The tulips, on the other hand, were first imported into Holland as far back as the sixteenth century, and their bulbs were even used as money at one point. I think it's why I love Europe. I never get tired of the centuries-old architecture and history."

"I need to come back one day when I have time to explore."

She stopped along the edge of the canal and looked up at him. "My father's missing, and I'm babbling about flowers. I just don't know how to deal with this."

"We need resources." Levi paused, clearly as desperate for answers as she was. "I have a friend who might be able to help us without involving the authorities."

"Who?"

"He's an old military buddy who runs a multinational corporation. He's the one who set up our company's risk assessment. Because a lot of his employees travel internationally and regularly do business in hot spots, he's able to handle crisis management and kidnapping and extortion threats."

"And you think he could put an end to this?"

"I think it's worth trying."

Kayla hesitated, still not willing to risk her father's life by getting someone else involved. "Let's check out Mercy's apartment first. If she's not there, we'll talk about calling your friend."

On any other day, Levi would have loved exploring the city. While he'd traveled extensively, Amsterdam had never been one of the cities he'd visited. The canals, old bridges covered with parked bicycles, the tall old houses...

He glanced at Kayla's profile as they headed toward the tram, not surprised at all that she'd ended up here working with formerly trafficked women. She'd always been compassionate, with a heart for others. And it seemed that all these years later, that compassion had only grown.

There was only one thing he wasn't sure how to handle. If she didn't agree to get help, he was going to have to consider doing it without her blessing. Because he knew enough about the situation to realize that they were in way over their heads. If they didn't get support from the authorities, the chances of her father's abductors making good on their threat rose substantially.

"Do you think they're out there watching us?" she asked, rubbing her elbow.

"It's possible."

They could be anyone. The man standing on the corner carrying a briefcase. The twentysomething sailing past them on a bike. They could be in the crowd watching the street performers or drinking coffee next to the canal. Absolutely anyone could be watching them. Stalking them.

He stopped beside Kayla in front of a blue-and-white tram; she quickly paid the fare for him, then scanned her ticket in front of a card reader. They headed toward the back of the tram, past blue chairs and a handful of passengers. As far as he could tell, no one was paying attention to them, but there was no way to be sure.

"Do you have any idea why someone would target Mercy in particular?" he asked as they slid into a couple of empty seats.

"She never spoke much about her past, though there was a man she mentioned once that she was afraid of. It sounded to me as if he was obsessed with her, but I have no idea who he was or what he looked like. I don't even have a name."

"How long has she been with your program?"

"She came to us about three months ago, originally from Nigeria. She came to us broken but eventually decided to stay and work with the program."

"So you're one of her mentors."

The automated voice on the tram announced their destination.

"This is our stop."

Five minutes later, they entered an apartment building and walked up a steep set of stairs to the third-story apartment. Kayla knocked on the door of number five.

Nothing.

"I'm assuming no one's home. The girls have a class tonight and normally aren't back until after eight," she said, knocking again on the door. "I have a key, but I never thought I might have to use it. Not for this."

When no one answered the second knock, she pulled the key from her bag and opened the door.

Kayla froze in the doorway. "Levi…they've already been here."

Levi stepped into the space behind her. The small living room and kitchen area had been trashed, leaving no doubt that whoever was after Mercy had made it here first.

"Why would they break in?"

"I'm assuming the same reason we're here. Trying to see if they can figure out where Mercy is in case motivating you doesn't work." He stepped over a pile of books scattered across the floor. "How many girls live here?"

"Five. Evi, my co-worker, told me that all the girls are accounted for except Mercy."

"And if they had Mercy, they wouldn't need your father." He stood in the middle of the room, not wanting to touch anything in case they decided to get the police involved. "I know this is tough, but you're doing some incredible things with these women. Don't forget that despite everything that's going on."

She shot him a half smile. "I won't, but

this…this is a reminder that these women had become nothing more than commodities."

"Why don't they just go to the police themselves?" he asked.

"Because prostitution is legal here, they are given contracts, but then they have to pay them back and the terms are impossible." She caught his gaze. "The girl that was recently found dead? She was convinced she couldn't go to the police because they weren't to be trusted and nothing we said could change that. I don't want that to happen to Mercy."

He followed her as she walked through the living room toward one of the bedrooms.

"This is Mercy's room," Kayla said. "She shares it with one of the other girls."

A couple of the dresser drawers weren't completely shut. There was a pile of clothes on the floor between the two twin beds, and the closet clearly had been gone through.

"Mercy doesn't have a lot of things, so while I'm not 100 percent sure, it looks to me like she left in a hurry. Her suitcase is gone, along with her toothbrush and other personal things." Kayla turned to Levi. "She had to have known someone was after her. And when they couldn't find her, they went to plan B."

"But why didn't she call one of you?"

"I don't know," she said.

"Has she been acting strange? Jumpy?"

"No…nothing that I noticed."

"Where might she have gone if she were scared?"

"Normally, she would have called me or Evi."

"What about other friends in the city?"

"I don't think she has many. Most of the girls don't make friends. They're slow to trust. That sense of survival isn't easy for them to shake."

"So we have to figure out where she might have gone," he said. "Because if we do, we'll have a chance at finding her and your father."

The floor creaked above them.

"What's up there?" he asked.

Kayla shook her head. "There's an attic you can access via a staircase in the back of the house. We're planning to remodel it and make it into a fourth bedroom eventually, but for now, it's just used for storage."

"Mercy could be hiding up there." Levi started for the steep staircase. "Or it's become the perfect hiding place for whoever trashed the apartment."

He ran up the stairs, hoping he was wrong and it was Mercy. But Kayla had hinted at what these people could do. As far as he could tell, murder wasn't just a threat. It was a line they wouldn't hesitate to cross if they didn't get what they wanted.

He stepped off the staircase and onto the attic floor. A figure lunged forward at him, swinging a knife and winging Levi's upper arm in the process. He took a step back, knowing he had to assume that the intruder wanted to kill him. He could see it in his eyes. Hand-to-hand combat had completely different rules from a shoot-out, and he had no weapon. And while the best defense might be to run, he wasn't going to risk Kayla's life in the process. His only option at the moment was to subdue the intruder.

The man faced him from the center of the dusty attic that contained a few dozen boxes, mattresses and a few pieces of furniture. He was taller by a good three to four inches and at least twenty pounds heavier, giving Levi another disadvantage.

There was no time to think, only to avoid the man's next lunge. Levi ducked to miss the move, but from the determined look on the man's face it seemed clear he hadn't expected them to show up. With the only option to fight or lead the intruder into a possible encounter with Kayla, Levi grabbed a small coffee table, braced it in front of himself and charged.

FOUR

Kayla hesitated as Levi disappeared up the staircase ahead of her toward the attic. Maybe she'd made the wrong call insisting they didn't alert the authorities, because they clearly needed all the help they could get. Her father's life depended on it. But on the other hand, they had legitimate reasons for following the orders of her father's abductors. She knew enough about the men who had trafficked Mercy to know they weren't people to cross and they weren't afraid to follow through with threats. She'd seen firsthand what people like them did to their victims.

And now she was seeing their destructive lifestyle affect her own family all over again.

God, please... I can't let them hurt my father.

She drew in a sharp breath and squeezed her eyes shut for a second, willing the dark memories to disappear. Authorities had found her sister in a filthy room, draped across the bed. Fifteen years old and her life had ended by those who'd forced her into the sex trade.

And now, if they didn't stop them this time, Mercy could end up being yet another victim. She wasn't going to let this happen.

Someone shouted from the attic above. Glass shattered. Shoving aside her fears, she drew in a deep breath and took the stairs two at a time, trying to calm the terror racing through her.

Seconds later, she stepped onto the cluttered attic floor. The intruder stood ten steps in front of her, swinging at Levi with a knife. She watched the blade slice down Levi's arm. A trail of red followed. She fought to catch her breath. They had no weapons. No easy way to stop this man. But she had to do something.

"Levi?"

"Kayla…get out of here. Now."

She heard his words but kept searching for a weapon. Ducking under one of the wooden beams running the length of the room, she grabbed a broken chair, picked it up, then ran forward and slammed it into the man's side. Pushing away the chair, he lunged at her with the knife. But the distraction had been enough. Levi moved closer to the man, disarming him in one fluid motion.

The man wasn't finished. He swung around in the small space. Kayla turned to avoid him, but she wasn't fast enough as he ran into her, knocking her into one of the low ceiling beams. She heard Levi shout as stars exploded into the darkness around her.

"Kayla?"

She couldn't breathe. Couldn't move. She forced her eyes open. She needed to get up. She could hear someone tearing down the stairs. They needed to go after him and find out who he was. Find out why he was in the girls' apartment.

"Levi?"

"Kayla... Kayla, I'm right here. Can you open your eyes?"

She groaned softly as her eyes blinked open. Levi hovered over her, fear clear in his eyes. He should be running after the man.

"He's getting away."

"It doesn't matter. Are you okay?"

She mentally went through her body—arms, legs, torso... The only thing that seemed to hurt was her head. "You always said I owed you for saving my life that day when we encountered that bull. Now I guess

I owe you again, but in the meantime, he got away. I'm sorry."

"Forget it. I just need to make sure you're okay."

"I'm fine. Really." She reached up and touched the back of her head, then slowly turned over on her side. "I think I'll just have a goose egg."

He was studying her eyes. She squirmed, far too close to those mesmerizing blue eyes of his.

"What are you doing?"

"Checking to see how much damage he did."

"I said I was fine."

"I'll be the judge of that. Your pupils seem normal along with your eye movement, and your speech seems normal as well."

"Thank you, Dr. Cummings."

"Funny, but I'm serious. How's your vision? Anything blurry?"

"No, because really, Levi, I'm okay."

She breathed in his spicy cologne. Fought the urge to reach up and touch a strand of his blond hair. He was hovering way too close.

"I need to take you to a doctor—"

"No," she said. "I just need a minute or two for my head to clear. Then I'll stand up."

He complied while she looked around the

room. The knife lay on the floor a couple feet from where she'd fallen. And that wasn't all that was there. "What do you think he was doing here?"

Nothing was making sense anymore.

He picked up a metal box and opened it. "Looks like spy gear. Audio recorders... And it's not cheap. Looks like he was planning to do a bit of surveillance if we didn't come and interrupt things."

"Why now?" she asked.

"Maybe they're not convinced we can find Mercy ourselves. Maybe they saw this as a backup plan to finding Mercy, by listening to the girls' conversations."

She waited for her head to stop spinning before she let him help her up, once again trying to ignore his nearness. Maybe she just needed some fresh air.

"I need to find another place for the girls to stay until all of this is over."

"What about the knife?" he asked. "It might have fingerprints on it that could lead to whoever's behind this."

"I suggest we report the break-in to the police, but leave out the abduction. At least for now. With my father's life at stake I don't want to risk it."

He glanced toward the door. "Do you think you can make it back downstairs?"

She nodded, knowing he was still worried. Knowing he wanted to protect her. But she wasn't sure he could put an end to what was happening to her this time.

"You're hurt as well," she said once they reached the bottom of the stairs. She reached up and touched his shirt where blood had stained the sleeve.

"It's nothing. I'll clean it up later."

She knew he wanted to shrug it off like it really was nothing. She knew he was already trying to figure out their next move. It was how he worked. How he'd served his country. He gathered information and came up with the most logical plan. But this time her father's life was on the line, and it terrified her.

And then there was Mercy. Kayla's entire world was focused on saving these girls.

He moved to the sink, wet a couple of paper towels and tried to clean up his arm.

"Stop," she said, crossing the floor. "You're just making a bigger mess."

She studied the three-inch-long cut, thankful it wasn't deep enough to need stitches, then ripped off the already torn sleeve to make it easier to clean. "Sorry, but this is going to sting."

"You know this is—was—my favorite shirt."

"I don't remember you being so vain."

He let out a chuckle, but all she could think about was that at least they were both alive. And that they had to figure out a way to make sure her father and Mercy stayed alive as well.

"Thankfully the knife barely nicked you. You would have needed stitches if he'd done any more damage, but as it is, I think you'll be okay as long as I can drum up some antibiotic cream and some sort of bandage."

"How's your head now?"

"I think I'm feeling clearheaded again." She glanced at the clock above the kitchen sink. It was already after seven. And they still had no idea where Mercy was.

She dug around in one of the cabinets. "I remember a first-aid kit… Here it is."

She pulled out a strip of gauze, a bandage with some tape and a tube of medicine.

"What is that?" he asked, pointing to the gel in her hand.

"The closest Dutch version of Neosporin I've found. No antibiotic, but it will help it heal."

"I'll take your word for it."

A minute later, she was finished. "So now that you're patched up, what's next?"

"We have to figure out where Mercy would

go. Who else does she trust? Where would she run if she was afraid for her life?"

The handle of the front door rattled. If they were back…

Levi grabbed the knife out of a wooden block on the kitchen counter, then headed for the front door, wishing he were better armed.

Seconds later a young woman, tall with dark hair and green eyes, appeared in the doorway with a backpack slung across her shoulder.

"Levi, wait…" Kayla quickly stepped between him and the girl. "This is Ana. She's one of the girls who lives here."

"Kayla…" Ana glanced around the living room then back to the two of them. "My key got stuck in the door. What…what's going on?"

"There was a break-in," Kayla said.

Levi followed the girl's gaze to his scraped-up arm before she spoke. "A break-in? What did they steal?"

"We don't think they stole anything. We think they were looking for someone."

"What do you mean?"

Kayla glanced at Levi before answering the question. "Mercy's missing and someone's trying to find her."

"Missing?" Ana's face paled as she sank onto the couch, dumping her backpack on the floor. "He's still looking for her, isn't he?"

Levi took a step forward. "Who?"

Ana shook her head. "I don't know. I just know that Mercy's been scared. For a couple weeks now, she's been screening her calls, leaving at different times every morning to go to work and making sure no one follows her."

Kayla sat down beside her. "Why didn't she tell me? That's why we're here. To help. To make sure something like this doesn't happen."

Ana rubbed her palms against the worn couch. "I know, but she was scared and didn't know what to do. She trusted you, but she was afraid she was imagining things."

"And if she was right? If someone was following her?" Kayla asked.

"She was afraid you would get the police involved."

"Why is she afraid of the police?" Levi asked.

Ana hesitated at the question.

"It's okay. He's here to help," Kayla said.

"Where she comes from—where most of us come from—the police are often a part of what's happening. Everyone takes the money and looks the other way. They are not on your side. That might not be true here, but sometimes…sometimes it's just easier to run."

"And the men who originally took Mercy were experts on feeding that fear," Kayla said.

Levi sat down on a small ottoman across from Kayla and Ana. Some of the pieces of the puzzle from what Kayla had told him earlier were coming together. While it might not have been smart to ignore their emergency plan, a part of him could understand why Mercy had run.

"When's the last time you saw Mercy?" Kayla asked.

"This morning." Ana stared straight ahead. The fear in her eyes signaled the fact that she knew it could have been any of them living in this apartment whose lives could be in danger. "She was getting ready for work."

"Did she seem upset?"

"Not upset. Distracted, maybe."

"Why?"

"She didn't talk about it much, but she was terrified her former pimp was going to track her down. I tried to assure her that she was safe now, but I don't think she believed me. I guess we all have a hard time believing that this new life is for real. That we won't just wake up and find that it's all been a dream."

"Do you have a name for the pimp?"

"Nicu, I think. He has a brother who works with him, but I don't remember his name."

"The name sounds familiar. I brought her file with me." Kayla dug in her backpack, pulled out Mercy's file and handed it to Levi. "I'd like you to go through it. It's mainly background information and interviews. See if there's something we can use that might help us find her."

"Isn't this information confidential?" he asked, catching her gaze.

"Normally yes, but let's say I'm hiring you as a consultant. I don't think I could do much better than a decorated army intelligence officer."

"Then I accept." He caught the relief in her eyes as he flipped open the file. "So Nicu—assuming that's who took her—was never arrested?"

"No." Kayla's brow furrowed at the question before she turned back to Ana. "Is there anything else you can think of that might help us find her?"

"She was receiving text messages from him. He wanted to see her. It was like he was…obsessed with her."

"Did you see any of the messages?"

"A couple of them. But she never wanted to

talk about it. I don't think she wanted any of us to know what was really going on."

"Do you know what was going on?"

"From the text I saw, he was angry that she left. Wanted her back."

Enough to target the one person he believed could find Mercy.

Ana glanced at the door. "What if they come back?"

"I intend to make sure you all are safe, Ana." Kayla's voice sounded calm. Soothing. "Why don't you quickly grab any personal items you might need for the next day or two for you and the other girls. I'll call a friend of mine who drives a taxi to take you to the center. I'll have Evi and Abel meet you there and ensure you and the other girls are safe tonight. Just as a precaution," she added.

Kayla picked up her phone as Ana left the room and quickly dialed the taxi.

"There are a couple bedrooms with bunk beds set up at our offices that we use as a transition space. They'll be safe there until this is over," she said once she'd hung up. She started straightening up the mess the intruder had left behind. "I'll also have Evi talk with each of the girls in person. See if Mercy said something to one of them that might help answer some of the questions we have."

Levi nodded. While he knew today had shaken Kayla, dealing with a crisis clearly came automatically to her.

"I think we need to let the police know about the break-in," Levi said, flipping open the file she'd given him.

"I can have Evi file a report, but I still don't think we can get the authorities involved with everything that's going on."

"I agree."

She picked a pile of books up off the floor and turned to him. "When's the last time you ate?"

Levi glanced at his watch, surprised at how late it was. "Let's see… Airplane food about five this morning."

"I'd rather not stay here. I know of a restaurant that's not far where we can grab soup and a sandwich. I'll call Evi and give her an update, and then we can go through Mercy's file and see if we can come up with something."

Fifteen minutes later Ana was on her way across town in a taxi, and they were sitting in the back of a little café offering homemade soups, sandwiches and cakes. They'd walked the long way, weaving between shops and up and down side streets to ensure they weren't followed, stopping only once to buy Levi a new shirt. But in the dark he couldn't guarantee that Nicu—or whoever was behind this—wasn't still out there. And as calm as Kayla had been with Ana, it was clear she was shaken up.

As soon as the waitress had taken their orders—spicy jalapeño-chicken sandwiches and fries served with mayonnaise, curry ketchup and some kind of peanut sauce—he continued reading through Mercy's file.

"Her story is pretty much like most of the girls we work with, though they come from different countries with equally horrifying stories. Mercy was working selling pineapple on the road when she met her *maman*."

"Her *maman*?" Levi glanced up from the file. "I might need a few blanks filled in before I read any more. Tell me what typically happens before the girls get to you."

"It's the word for madams in Nigeria. They usually work through local pimps— like Nicu—or sometimes the Mafia. Mercy thought she was doing something that would help her family back home. Her *maman* promised a job working in a European shop."

"And instead she ended up trapped in a world with no way out."

"Exactly."

The waitress set down their plates of food,

then asked if they needed anything else before she left. Levi dunked a fry into the traditional Dutch peanut sauce Kayla had recommended.

"It's not bad, is it?"

"I'm hungry enough that it just might grow on me."

Kayla let out a soft laugh. Her smile made him wish he could see her in a different setting under different circumstances. A chance to take her out and get to know her again without the stress of the situation.

"Everything these people do is well planned out," Kayla continued, ignoring her food for the moment. "In Africa, the traffickers usually go to remote villages where there are no options for these girls. No work. No education. In turn the girls believe they have nothing to lose. When they find out the truth about what job is really waiting for them, they don't see a way out."

"No identity papers would reinforce their fear of local authorities."

"Exactly." Kayla picked up a fry, dabbed it in her sauce, then set it back down on the plate without eating it. "Typically a *maman* holds over the girls the debt for the plane ticket, food costs and rent. And in return, they are forced to earn their keep by selling their bodies."

"Until you—and others like you—come along."

"Yes, but what frustrates me is that for every Mercy we try to save, there are dozens more out there still trapped. It's a lucrative business that won't be stopped simply by targeting the traffickers, or even by saving the girls. The only way to put an end to it is by stopping those who demand their services.

"I can't stop thinking about Lilly." Kayla took a sip of her water, her food still untouched as she continued talking. "Her story isn't that different from Mercy's. She wanted something different. Something more. She met this woman who told her she was a model scout and worked as an agent for dozens of girls. Lilly came home ecstatic."

"And your parents?"

"They did some research. The woman had a professional website and connections to other people in the industry. On the surface everything checked out. Then the woman convinced Lilly that if she moved to Paris, she'd have more opportunities to model, but my parents told her no. Told her that she was too young and needed to finish school. They pulled her out of the agency, but Lilly…she could be stubborn. She hated living in such a small town and was convinced that she was going to miss her one big opportunity if she walked away."

"Which she believed would happen if she stayed in Potterville."

Kayla nodded as the raw memories swirled around her.

"There was a huge blowup between her and my parents. The next day, Lilly went missing, and my family was suddenly sitting in the living room talking with the FBI about a possible abduction. They were able to trace her to Houston, but she'd disappeared along with five other girls. That's when we found out the terrifying truth that it's far more common than we might imagine for men—and sometimes women—to pose as modeling agents in order to traffic women. And if they are able to get them out of the country, American women typically can be sold for more."

"Did they make it out of the country?"

"Three of them did. A fourth girl was flagged and picked up at the airport in Atlanta by the local authorities. To this day we're not sure why they kept Lilly in the States, then killed her. They found her during a huge sting by the authorities. There were over fifty arrests, and twice that many young girls res-

cued that day. It was a huge bust. And then
they found Lilly. But it was too late. The au-
topsy said she died of a drug overdose, more
than likely forced on her to keep her in line."

"I'm so, so sorry, Kayla."

Her phone rang, and she grabbed it from
the table. He listened to the one-sided conversation, trying to figure out whom she was
talking to. Her frown deepened. Whoever it
was, it wasn't good news.

"Kayla?"

He watched her drop the phone back onto
the table in front of her. Her frown deepened.

"What is it?"

"I have a contact at the police department.
He…he's helped us before with different situations we've had to deal with." She drew in a
deep breath before continuing. "A Jane Doe
was just brought into the morgue. They want
me to come in and see if I can identify her.
They found my business card in her pocket."

Levi caught the tremor in her voice. "And
you think it might be Mercy?"

A shadow crossed Kayla's face. "If Mercy
is dead, what happens to my father?"

FIVE

Kayla stopped outside the cold, sterile air of the morgue, unsure where she was going to find the courage to step through the door. It wasn't the first time she'd been here. The last time she'd worked with the police, she'd been called in to identify one of the victims. Seeing the familiar face of one of the girls they'd worked with lying on the slab had ended up haunting her dreams for months.

Just like Lilly.

Hands clenched beside her, she continued the prayer she'd started before leaving Mercy's apartment, begging God to put an end to this by somehow saving both Mercy and her father. But the fact remained that someone wasn't going home tonight. Instead they were lying there on the other side of the door. A Jane Doe. Kayla had always known her job held risks. They were dealing with men who

had no moral compass. But ending this way…
this was what she was desperate to stop.

She turned to the attendant who had
brought them down here. "Where did you
find her?"

"Someone saw her floating in one of the
canals and tried to save her, but she was already dead. There was no ID on her, and so
far we haven't been able to match her to any
missing-person report."

And so they'd called her, hoping she might
be able to ID the woman.

Levi squeezed her hand, making her thankful she hadn't had to come alone. "Are you
ready to go inside?"

"I'm not sure I'll ever be ready for this,
but yes." She nodded at the attendant, then
walked into the room behind him.

Kayla hesitated while he pulled back the
sheet covering the woman's body. She shut
her eyes for a moment before taking a step,
then gazed at the body. Her breath caught.
There was nothing familiar about the dark-
skinned girl who couldn't be more than sixteen or seventeen. Her hair was pulled back
and her eyes were closed as if she were sleeping.

Kayla pressed the back of her hand against
her mouth and shook her head. "It's not Mercy."

"Are you sure?" the attendant asked before covering her up again.

"I'm sure. I've never seen this girl before."

Tears flooded her eyes. She hated the relief, but any relief she felt was combined with a deep hurt. This girl had to have a family. Someone who cared about her. Someone who would notice when she didn't come home. That alone was heartbreaking.

But it wasn't Mercy or one of the other girls she'd worked with. Which meant they still had a chance of finding Mercy alive.

"I need to go," she said, taking a step backward. "Thank you for calling me."

She pushed open the heavy door and stepped out into the dark hallway. The smell of death hovered along the green walls of the building, threatening to suffocate her.

Levi grasped her elbow. "Let's get you out of here."

A moment later Levi had led her out of the building, his hand still protective on her arm as they stepped out into the darkness.

"I'm sorry," she said.

"Don't be, but you're shaking."

She hesitated before responding. "I've been here before. It's a chilling reminder that we can't save them all. She had my card, Levi, and yet I don't even recognize her."

"This wasn't your fault."

"I know."

But if the girl had called her, they might have been able to save her. Instead, they'd lost her. And if they didn't figure out where Mercy was, they were going to lose her—and Max—as well.

"You said you've been here before?"

She nodded. "I told you about the girl who was murdered three months ago. They called me to the morgue to identify her body. I still remember every detail of that night. The sound of my boots hitting the cement floor. The flicker of the fluorescent light sputtering above me. The smell of bleach. I remember standing over the body when they pulled down the sheet so I could look at her face. The shot of horror when I recognized her. I couldn't believe it was Kim. She'd been doing so well."

The outside temperatures had dropped, leaving a damp chill running through Kayla's body. She tried to push away the haunting memories. Memories that kept her up at night. Memories that only made her determined to fight harder to save these girls.

Her phone rang. She glanced at the caller ID. Evi. She'd almost forgotten she'd promised to let her coworker know what they discovered at the morgue.

"Was it her?" Evi asked before Kayla could even say hello.

"No. I didn't recognize her."

"I'm so sorry you had to do that."

"Me, too. Have you found out anything from the girls?"

"Not yet. Whatever Mercy was planning, she kept it to herself." There was a long pause on the line. "And I've done what I can to reassure the girls that they're safe, but they're scared."

"I know. Listen, Levi and I are on our way to the office right now and should be there in about twenty minutes. I plan to talk to the girls as well. We need to figure out where Mercy would go if she was in trouble."

"Okay, just promise you'll be careful."

Kayla hung up the phone. She blew out a deep breath as they started walking again. "I know we need to head to the center, but can we walk partway? There are still a lot of people out, so it should be safe. I just need to clear my head for a few minutes."

"Sure," he said, glancing at his watch.

Restaurants were serving the dinner crowd. People sat outside drinking coffee and eating despite the chilly temperatures. To their left, the canal was lit up with streetlamps and shops next to an old row of canal houses.

"Some people call this the Venice of the north." The air was clearing her head, and for the moment, talking was the only way she knew how to cope with the situation. "I went on a tour of the city when I first arrived. Amsterdam's actually built on millions of wooden poles and has over a hundred kilometers of canals."

"I can't say that I knew that."

"There are also hundreds of bridges."

"What about bicycles?" he asked, skirting out of the way of one. "There's got to be thousands of those."

She let out a low laugh. "I've heard that there are actually more bicycles than people living in the city."

"Maybe when all of this is over you can show me a few of your favorite places."

"I'd like that."

When this was over.

Is it ever going to be over, God?

It was as if it were happening all over again. With Lilly... With Kim...

"Kayla?"

She felt his hand against her arm and looked up.

"Are you okay?"

She started to say yes, then shook her head. "Honestly? No. I'm not okay. I realized when I took this job that there were aspects of it that were potentially dangerous. But that isn't what scares me the most. I stepped into my position with my eyes wide-open. It was my choice. But these girls… The girls we help didn't choose this life. Mercy didn't choose this life."

She turned to face him, tears pooling in her eyes. She needed to stay strong. Needed to keep her head clear, but all she could see was her father and Mercy lying on that slab in the morgue if they didn't stop these men. And they couldn't let that happen.

"Hey." He tilted up her chin with his hand until she was looking at him underneath a streetlight. "We're going to figure this out. I promise."

"And if we don't?"

He shook his head. "We have to. There's too much at stake."

He pulled her against his chest and wrapped his arms around her, a hedge of safety surrounding her. She drew in a deep breath, forcing herself to both focus and relax. Because he was right. The stakes were too high for them not to figure this out.

She took a step backward and glanced up at

Levi, surprised at how thankful she was that he was here. And how safe he made her feel. She might have tried to push him away when he'd attempted to save her all those years ago, but deep down he'd always been that handsome hero she'd looked up to. Always a tower of strength, and over the years, that part of him hadn't changed. He'd always been the responsible oldest son, the rescuing big brother, there to pick up the pieces.

But the last thing she needed right now was a distraction, and certainly not with her ex-fiancé's brother. The countdown wasn't stopping just because they hadn't found Mercy.

"You're still shaking."

"I'm freezing."

"We just passed a shop selling hot chocolate."

She nodded. It was more than just the weather, but she could use something to take off the chill. A minute later, she took the hot chocolate he handed her then took a sip, burning the tip of her tongue in the process.

"What are you thinking?" he asked, drinking the coffee he'd bought for himself as they headed toward the tram.

"I'm worried about what we're supposed to do if we end up finding Mercy. Even if we find her, we can't exchange her."

"I know, but if she can help us locate the men behind this, we might have a chance."

"You have to have some advice." She blew on her hot chocolate, then took another sip, feeling the warmth of the drink seep through her. "You dealt with hostage situations and negotiated in your line of work when you were in the military."

"Yes, but this is different."

"Different how?"

Levi tried to analyze her question as he studied the street scene around them. A man wearing a wool hat walked a dozen meters behind them on the other side of the street. He'd seen the man a few minutes earlier but hadn't been able to determine yet if he was following them. For now, he'd simply have to keep his guard up.

"For one, we don't have any tactical backup. And now I've seen what they can do, not only to these girls, but to anyone who gets in their way. They're ruthless and don't care who they hurt."

He drank the rest of his coffee, then dumped his empty cup into a trash can. Or maybe what was different was that Kayla was the one who'd been caught in the cross fire this time. Not that that should matter. Being here was never supposed to be personal, but for some reason it was becoming just that.

His evaluation of the situation, though, had been correct. They were up against an unknown enemy, and moving ahead without sufficient information. All of which further legitimized Kayla's concerns. Finding Mercy didn't guarantee her father's safety, because an exchange wasn't an option. A situation that somehow felt all too familiar.

When he'd been responsible for his team, he'd known that if he made one mistake, one wrong call, he could end up sacrificing all their lives. It was what had gotten him up in the mornings, because he felt that there was significance to what he was doing no matter how hard the assignment. He was doing it for his country. For freedom. Until the day he'd found himself in a situation where even with all the intel he'd processed and the strategies they'd put into place, it hadn't been enough to stop five soldiers from being caught behind enemy lines.

He glanced at Kayla, who'd become quiet and focused as they hurried toward the tram, his hand still wrapped around hers. Her job wasn't much different than his had been. She felt the responsibility of ensuring the safety of these girls she worked with. Not only to bring them out of a difficult situation, but to ensure that they stayed safe. He'd seen the intensity in her eyes and heard the passion in her voice. She wasn't going to give up on finding her father, but neither would she sacrifice Mercy. And right now, he had no idea how to help her do that.

She stopped at a red light and blew out a puff of air. "How do we fix this?"

He wanted to tell her not to worry. That they'd find a way to fix this. But after everything that had happened, he wasn't sure anymore.

"What do you think we should do besides interview the girls?" she asked when he didn't answer.

He tried to choose his words carefully as they passed a well-lit café. A glance to the right showed no sign of the man in the hat, but he still wasn't ready to dismiss the fact that someone could be following them.

"This isn't a typical hostage situation. There is no one to negotiate with while we gather more intel. I can't talk to them, or listen to them and find a way to get them to trust me. They don't work that way."

So what was the answer?

It wasn't the first time he'd considered bringing in outside help. Since his return, he'd had half a dozen job offers from risk-management companies. The number of international kidnappings continued to rise, particularly in Africa and the Middle East. Both extortion and ransom had become big businesses. But in this situation, he was still debating if hiring an expert was an option they should take.

"All I know to do is stick with our plan," he said finally. "We talk to the girls, figure out where Mercy might have run and hopefully find her. And if we can find her, we hope she can help us lead us to where they might have your father."

He caught the look of frustration on Kayla's face as they stepped onto the blue-and-white tram. He studied the handful of passengers, the uneasy feeling he'd had all the way here intensifying. They were too out in the open. Too vulnerable. He never should have let her leave the apartment, and yet doing nothing wasn't going to help them, either.

"How many more stops?" he asked.

"Three," she said, as he sat down next to her in the back of the tram. "I've been wanting to ask about your father."

Her question caught him off guard as he forced his mind to momentarily switch gears, his senses still on high alert.

"Between my father's health and my brother's prison sentence, my parents have had a hard couple of years."

"What exactly is wrong with your father?"

"Prostate cancer. He's doing better after a few major changes to his diet and a list of other things, but it's never far from our minds."

"And he's the reason you returned to Potterville."

He glanced at his leg that still held a piece of shrapnel. "That and an ambush in the Middle East. I didn't have much of a choice."

"You miss it, don't you? The military?"

The tram stopped, and he studied the passengers getting on. In any other situation he would be soaking up every moment with Kayla. Enjoying their conversation while getting to know her again after all these years. But today…today all he could think about was keeping her safe.

"It's been hard to find my feet as a civilian again," he said, finally answering her question.

"Do you ever think about going back?"

"Well, I don't see myself sitting behind a desk for the rest of my life. Though for now, my only goal is to keep things running in the company for my father until he's ready to take over again. After that… I haven't decided."

"My father told me you're good at what you're doing right now."

"There are things I love about my job. Working with people and knowing that we're making a difference to the community. But like I said, sitting behind a desk all day or going to meeting after meeting…that isn't exactly my thing."

She wrapped her fingers around his arm. "I'm scared, Levi. Scared of how all of this is going to turn out."

He squeezed her hand. "I know."

She nodded as the tram started slowing down again. "We can get off here."

"How close are we to your office?"

"Three blocks."

They stepped off the tram, then headed down the street. A car turned the corner slowly, coming toward them from behind. They were in a quieter neighborhood now. Someone flew past them on a bike, but beyond that and the car, the street was empty.

"We need to get out of here," he said, trying to squelch the uneasiness that had taken over. "We need to be somewhere less isolated."

"There's a row of shops up ahead to our left. Our offices are located just past them."

They picked up their pace toward the lighted area, but the car made the same left turn. His stomach clenched as the car slowed behind them. Something was off. This time there was no doubt they were being followed.

He grabbed her hand and started walking faster.

"Levi."

"I think they found us."

"They've already got my father. Why would they need us?"

"I don't know."

Squeezing his fingers tighter around her hand, he started running.

The car engine roared behind them. He wasn't imagining things this time.

"Levi…"

"Keep running."

The street was deserted. He could hear the faint strains of a radio playing from one of the apartments above them, but with the cold, windows were closed and most people were bundled up inside their apartments. And they were still too far away from the lit-up area ahead.

Houses framed either side of the road. The vehicle screeched to a stop in front of them, blocking off the road. Unless they turned around, there was nowhere to run.

Two men in black emerged from the car. Levi caught the gleam of a gun in the glow of the streetlight, then moved Kayla behind him as they backed up. She grabbed his arm and screamed.

"Shut up or I will shoot you."

Levi eyed the gun. Getting in the vehicle with them couldn't be an option. They'd lose any remaining control over the situation. His only choice was to try to fight his way out.

One of the men approached them from the right. He belted the man with his elbow, then reached for the weapon. But he was no match for two armed men. They grabbed him and Kayla, locked their hands behind them and roughly placed blindfolds over their eyes. Levi felt a stab of pain shoot through his head, and he stumbled forward.

Then complete darkness surrounded him.

SIX

Kayla gasped for a breath beneath the confines of the blindfold covering her eyes. Panic set in. She had no idea how long it had been since they had grabbed her and Levi off the street. All she really knew was that darkness felt as if it were closing in like a choking hand. Her hands were tied behind her back, making it difficult—if not impossible—to pull the blindfold off and take in her surroundings.

She prayed as she tried to loosen the cords securing her hands. Levi had to be here somewhere, and maybe her father as well. She had to find them. In the vehicle they'd been shoved into, she'd tried to figure out where they were being taken, but eventually she'd given up. She couldn't be sure how much time had passed, or how far they'd driven. There wasn't even any way to know for sure if Levi had been brought here as well.

What she did know was that this was no coincidence. Payback, perhaps, because they hadn't followed the rules? They might not have told the police what was going on, but they had gone to the government morgue. What was she supposed to tell them now? She had no idea where Mercy was, and no idea where to find her.

The unwanted image of her sister's body flashed in front of her. She tugged at the bindings around her wrists. Is this what the girls had felt when they'd realized who those men really were? She'd seen the fear in the eyes of the girls she'd worked with, heard the worry in their voices.

Kayla drew in a deep breath. Panicking over what could happen wasn't going to get her out of here. She needed to make a plan. Needed to figure out where she was and how to get out. She estimated they'd driven at least forty-five minutes, maybe an hour. Enough time to take them outside the city and into the surrounding countryside. They'd pulled her and Levi out of the vehicle, still blindfolded. He'd held on to her for as long as he could, until someone had pulled them apart. After that...all she knew was that she'd felt so tired and must have eventually fallen asleep.

Levi had tried to fight back, but she had

no idea if he'd been injured…or even if he was still alive, for that matter. She shook off the thought, trying not to think about a worst-case scenario. Because while her connection to Levi's family might have ended a long time ago, the thought of anything happening to him terrified her. And all she knew for sure was that she wished he was here with her right now. Since his unexpected arrival, he'd somehow become the quiet shelter in the storm. The steady rock holding her in place.

Not that she had any romantic feelings toward him. Not at all. Levi was nothing more than a familiar face. Someone from back home who had brought with him a pile of memories she wanted to forget. She'd almost become a part of his family once, and it hadn't ended well. There was no way she was going to fall for the older brother. Their intertwined past was simply too complicated.

She pushed aside the distracting thoughts, focusing instead on freeing herself from the blindfold. Thirty seconds later it finally slipped from her face, allowing her to see the sunlight streaming in from a window. She closed her eyes for a moment, then let them slowly adjust to the brightness.

The blindfold off, Kayla moved on to try to release the cords tightly binding her hands while she studied the large room for a clue as to where she was. The walls of the chilly room needed a fresh coat of paint, and there were sheets covering the sparse furniture. She didn't know much about architecture, but she had visited several stunning country estates outside Amsterdam. And from the surface, this room seemed similar in construction, with its tall ceiling and crown molding. Many of the estates surrounding the city had been built centuries ago as coveted destinations for relaxing in the country with their gardens and stunning architectural details. But this structure felt more like a prison than a place for an afternoon getaway.

Kayla turned her head as footsteps sounded outside the room. Her heart raced as the door creaked open to her left. She turned her head, and the fear that had been her companion over the last twenty-four hours escalated another notch as a tall figure stepped inside the room, his icy stare slicing right through her.

"You had to do this the hard way, didn't you?" he said hovering above her.

Kayla tried to swallow the fear. "Who are you?"

"That doesn't matter. What did you tell them?"

"Tell who?"

"The police." His frown deepened. "Because as I remember, you were told very explicitly not to talk with the police."

She shook her head. "I didn't tell them anything. We went to the morgue. That was all."

"Why?"

"To identify a body."

"And you expect me to believe that you or your boyfriend didn't happen to mention that someone has your father?"

She wanted to argue that Levi wasn't her boyfriend, but it didn't matter. She had a feeling he wasn't going to believe anything she said. She glanced at the door that was still open a crack, looking for escape, but at the moment there was clearly no way out.

"I received a call from a contact," she attempted to explain. "He asked to meet me at the morgue, so I did."

"Why?"

"He thought I might know who the girl was."

The man took a step back at her statement. "You thought it was Mercy."

She nodded, catching a flash of concern in the man's eyes.

He dropped his hands to his sides. "Was it her?"

"No."

Whatever had struck a nerve with the man a moment before had now vanished. A second man stepped into the doorway, then started speaking rapidly in a foreign language and motioned for him to step outside.

"I'll be back."

She tried to stop the panic as the two men argued about something in the hallway. Something was off. The look she'd caught in his eye when she'd told him why she was at the morgue. That split second of fear. Could he truly be concerned about Mercy? She had to have just imagined any hint of concern. Because something had propelled him to not only take her father, but now her and Levi. Was there something beyond a financial desire to take back his source of income?

The sound of heavy boots on the scuffed wooden floor pulled her from her thoughts once again. Both men now stood in front of her.

"I'm assuming you know why you're here?" the first man asked her, his voice laced with irritation.

She didn't answer the question immediately, taking time instead to study the men. From the language they'd been speaking, she guessed they were from Eastern Europe. Both had olive skin, square jaws and high cheekbones, and they looked similar enough to pass as brothers.

"You gave me twenty-four hours to find Mercy," she finally answered.

"Without going to the police."

"And I said I didn't."

He leaned in toward her. "You think this is a game?"

"Hardly. But if that's true, then tell me what you want with her. You've got a dozen girls who will take her place. Why not just leave her alone?"

"I don't remember asking your opinion. What I asked you to do is find her. Where is she?"

"I don't know. I need more time."

"Because your father's running out of time."

"Where is he? And Levi? Please tell me they're okay."

"They're both fine. For now. And I have some extra insurance if I need it. Levi Sinclair Cummings, CEO of an American manufacturing company, has to be worth a large chunk of cash—at least a couple million."

"So now you're into the kidnapping and ransom business?"

"I told you this was a bad idea." The other man said.

"Call it payback. Your little non-profit has done enough damage to my business."

"It's not a business, what you do," Kayla retorted. "It's human trafficking. These girls don't choose to work for you."

"Which really isn't any of your business. So here's the bottom line. Where is Mercy? Because I think you're lying to me, which isn't going to fare well for your father. Mercy trusts you. She's not going to just run away from the one person who she believes can help her."

Like she ran away from you?

"Here's what I think happened," he continued, his face now red with anger. "She knew I wanted her back, so now you've got her hidden in some little village along the sea, or maybe in some house in the country. But where she is really doesn't matter. I not only have you, but I have your father and now Levi. If you don't tell me where she is, I won't hesitate to kill both of them."

She turned her head away, fighting back the tears. Even if she did know where Mercy was, she couldn't just hand her over to this man. Not only were there no guarantees that they would let her father and Levi go, she knew without any doubts that Mercy would be caught in the cross fire.

There's no way out of this, God. I have no idea what to do.

It was like choosing whom to save. And if they happened to find Mercy before she did, she would no longer have the leverage she needed to keep any of them alive.

"You seem to have all the bases covered." She didn't try to hold back the anger in her voice.

"I always do."

Maybe, but one day she was going to ensure his entire operation was taken down.

"One more thing." Her abductor took a step back. A wicked smile crossed his face. "In case you're hesitating on doing what I say. About that girl you saw in the morgue tonight."

"I said it wasn't Mercy."

"I know that now. I just didn't expect them to find her so…quickly."

"She was one of your girls," Kayla said, feeling numb.

"She's not the only one who might end up in the canal. Just remember that. You hand over Mercy and no one dies—including Mercy. But cross me and both you and your friend will end up dead. Which means you better cooperate. And for starters, there's something you're going to do for me."

* * *

Levi opened his eyes with a start. His vision blurred as he stared above him at the cracks in the ceiling, trying to figure out where he was. He started to sit up, then winced at the sharp pain in the back of his head. Jaw stiffened, he lay back down on the hard flooring. From the curtainless window to his left, he could tell that the sun was already up, but he had no idea how long he'd been asleep.

The last thing he remembered was trying to fight off two armed men who'd attacked them after they got off the tram. An attack that obviously ended with a blow to his head. He started to reach up to feel his head, but his hands felt heavy. Weighted. Confusion hung over him for a minute, until he realized why he couldn't move. Both his hands and feet were tied.

He let out a deep sigh. There was no way to know at this point whether or not he had a concussion. All he did know was that the top of his head pounded and his entire body felt as if he had been in a fight. Which, from the snippets he could remember, he had been.

He weighed his limited options. The only way he was going to find Kayla was if he managed to get out of the room before the men came back for him. Which he knew they would eventually. Rolling over onto his side, Levi ignored the pain as he sat up so he could maneuver his arms beneath his body. Once his hands were in front of him, he started tugging on the thin cord with his teeth. His frustration mounted as he tried to work through the night's events in order to figure out where they might have brought him.

He shivered as he worked to loosen the cords. The temperature had continued to drop outside, filling the room with a cold draft. How had this happened? He'd come here to protect Kayla, and yet no matter how hard he'd fought, it hadn't been enough to stop their attackers and keep her safe. Fear seeped through him, bringing with it a wave of nausea. He'd come to Amsterdam to protect her, and now he didn't even know where she was.

I need Your help, God. I have to get out of here and find her.

The light from the window was just enough for him to make out the shadows of the room, empty except for a few pieces of old furniture and a couple of rugs. The crown molding and remnants of gold wallpaper told a different story, though, giving a hint to what the room might have once looked like.

Still working to loosen the cords, he tried

to picture the map of Amsterdam and the surrounding area that he'd studied on the plane. To the east of the city was water, and to the west, past Haarlem, was water as well. His mom had given him a list of day trips that he could take outside Amsterdam, assuming his trip was work related and he would want to see some of the countryside.

There were iconic windmills built to keep the country from flooding, tulip fields ready to bloom after winter was over, cheese markets and dozens of scenic places to bike alongside canals and eat fresh waffles. The in-flight magazine he'd thumbed through on his way here had talked about how rich merchants used to leave Amsterdam for extravagant estates built along the banks of the Rivers Amstel and Vecht in the summertime. And while this place might not be quite as grand, by the architecture he could tell it was both old and large. Which meant they had to be some distance from the city.

He shivered again. Instead of loosening the binding, he had somehow made it tighter, the ropes digging into his wrists, making his skin raw. He ignored the pain, focusing instead on the question that continued to trouble him. Why had they changed their mind from giving Kayla twenty-four hours to find Mercy, to grabbing them off the street? Something must have happened to prompt them to change the rules of the game.

But what?

His mind snapped back to the morgue where they'd gone to identify Jane Doe. The only thing that made sense was that their abductors had seen them go into the morgue, convincing them they were working with the police. Which had him worried. If these men were as dangerous as Kayla said they were—which he believed—they wouldn't hesitate to kill anyone who got in their way. Which also meant that at this point, more than likely both he and Max were simply pawns in this drama. Expendable pawns that at some point in the near future they would eliminate.

But despite the urgency of the situation, it was the image of Kayla that currently hovered the closest to the forefront of his mind. Because there was no use denying it. Seeing her again had opened up a flood of emotions he hadn't expected to feel. He thought he'd left behind any boyhood crushes years ago, burying them completely. And yet walking back into her life after all these years had only gone to prove that those feelings were far from dead. There was something about her that made him want to tell her he'd always cared about her. That seeing her again had made him want to turn back time to the day he'd blown any chance with her. That had always been his one regret. The one moment in time he'd never been able to erase.

The thought caught him off guard. It was ridiculous, really. How could he have feelings for a woman he didn't really know anymore? He hadn't seen her for almost two years, and even then he hadn't really spent any time with her. Neither of them were who they'd been when they were kids. Besides, things could never work out between them. It simply wasn't possible. She'd once planned on marrying his brother, and it didn't really matter that she didn't have feelings for Adam anymore. He wasn't falling for her again. Not after all these years. He could think of a dozen reasons why it was a bad idea.

Wasn't it?

The cords around his wrists finally loosened a quarter of an inch. Would he have flown halfway around the world for someone he didn't have feelings for? He tugged harder on one of the cords. The answer to the question seemed obvious. He'd always had a strong sense of duty. A need to fight for justice. But as true as that might be, that wasn't the entire truth. Because no matter how hard he tried to fight it, he'd never completely lost the feelings he'd always had for Kayla.

It was the reason he'd felt he had to protect her from his brother. The reason he'd come to Amsterdam in the first place. He just hadn't realized who the enemy was or what lengths they'd go to get what they wanted. But none of that really mattered at the moment. What mattered right now was finding a way to get loose so he could find Kayla.

A minute later, the cords around his wrists slackened and fell off. Another minute and the cord around his feet was off. Levi slowly stretched out his legs, then stood up, before going to the window. The property was clearly large, even from his limited vantage point. He could see a row of trees about a hundred feet from the house, and beyond that, a tall fence. Movement to the left shifted his attention. A couple of German shepherds roamed the property. Great. But he couldn't worry about that right now. He was going to have to tackle one problem at a time. Which meant his immediate priority was finding Kayla without getting caught.

Rubbing the raw patch on his skin, he headed for the door. The handle wouldn't budge. There had to be a way out. He started pulling open the drawers of the dresser to see if there was anything he could use. He stopped at the bottom drawer, which was filled with a bunch of miscellaneous junk, and dug through the contents. A few photographs, a pile of old newspaper, some coins and a handful of bobby pins…

Bingo.

Grabbing two of the pins, he headed back to the locked door. Using one of the pins as a tension wrench and the second as a pick, he started working the lock, thankful—not for the first time—for his military tactical training. All he had to do right now was find a way out of the room and save Kayla. He'd worry about Mercy and Kayla's father next.

Shouts from outside the room interrupted his concentration. Levi frowned, unsure if it was the same two men from earlier. Either way, the urgency of getting out of the room was growing. Clearly he wasn't the only person in the house. He felt the plug move and gently applied more force to the tension wrench.

Two minutes later, the door creaked open, and Levi stepped into the darkened hallway. He listened for the sound of voices but didn't hear anything anymore. He was going to move ahead with the assumption that Kayla was in this house, and more than likely Max was here as well. Because Kayla's life was in danger and he was running out of time.

SEVEN

Kayla hesitated at her abductor's request. Seconds seemed to stretch into minutes.

I can't do this, God.

"Apparently you didn't hear me," he said. "I want you to call Mercy and arrange to meet her."

She tugged on the edge of the frayed binding that secured her hands. She'd known it would come down to this at some point. The moment they forced her to choose. They expected her to just hand Mercy over to them. But she'd promised to help keep Mercy safe. How could she betray her now?

But if she didn't do what they were asking, what about her father and Levi?

She needed to find a way to escape, but that wasn't going to happen with the man standing right in front of her with a gun pointed at her. There was no way out.

"Nicu—" the other man said.

"Shut up, Andrei." Nicu kept his gaze fixed on Kayla.

"I've already called her a dozen times," she said, "but she won't pick up. I haven't found another way to reach her."

He took a step forward and pressed the muzzle of the gun under her chin. "Do you think this is a game? That your father's life isn't really in danger?"

Kayla felt her body tremble as she shook her head.

"Good, because somehow I don't think you understand how serious this is. I want you to call Mercy and tell her you need to see her. Tell her that you know she's in danger, and you have a plan to help."

"And then what happens? You show up and grab her?"

"Something like that."

"I won't do it."

He let out a low laugh. "You won't do it? Here's the thing. You aren't exactly in a place to bargain here. You have zero leverage. I have your boyfriend and your father, and I'm perfectly happy to use them to get what I want."

Kayla dug for every ounce of courage she could muster. Maybe if she stalled, Levi would escape and find her. He was still out there somewhere, and he had combat experience. Even if he couldn't help her, it wouldn't be long before someone noticed she was missing. Evi had been expecting her to come to the office to talk to the girls last night, which meant she'd probably already called the police.

Except no one knew where she was. She looked up and caught Nicu's stare. By the time anyone found her, it would probably be too late. And she was out of options.

"What if I don't help you?"

He held up his phone, showing her a string of photos. Levi holding her hand. Levi looking down at her beneath a streetlight, his eyes filled with worry. Her instincts had been right. They had been watched. Followed.

"That's simple," he said. "The local authorities are going to find the bodies of three foreigners in one of the canals. Though I'm assuming that's not what you want."

"And if Mercy doesn't respond to my call?"

"I know Mercy. She will eventually, because she's running out of options. She needs someone to go to and she trusts you. She can only run for so long on her own. She doesn't have any identity documents and little, if any, money… The bottom line is that she needs you."

"Why don't you just let her go? What does she—one girl—really matter to you?"

"None of those other girls are Mercy."

Kayla tried to read his expression. "No, but there are a dozen more girls who can take the place of Mercy. Why don't you just let her go before this gets out of hand and someone gets hurt? Or you get arrested? All you have to do is walk away."

"You're actually worried about my getting arrested?" He clapped his hands together slowly, his expression mocking her. "That's quite a performance, but you're not really worried about me. Because you can't win this. The only way to save your father—and yourself—is to give me Mercy. And I'm showing you how. It's that simple."

There was something about the way Nicu spoke about Mercy. This wasn't about just getting a piece of his property back. "You're in love with her, aren't you?"

She wasn't sure what he felt toward Mercy could actually be called love, but she needed a way to connect with him. A way to resolve all of this before someone got hurt. If that was even possible.

Nicu's glance dropped. "Mercy's different from the other girls. We understand each other."

"If she understood you, then why did she decide to leave?"

"We had a disagreement."

Kayla shook her head. "I know the kind of girls you target. Girls that don't have the strength to fight back for themselves. That was Mercy when I found her. You took the spark out of her eyes, because you made her do things she would never have done on her own in order to save her family from your threats."

"Everything these girls do is legal here, but you…you'll never understand what I do for them—"

"Understand what?" She knew she'd never be able to hold a rational conversation with him, but frustration pushed her forward. "That you're doing this because you love her? Because what you've done to her isn't love."

"Enough." Nicu slapped her cheek with the back of his hand. "I never asked for your opinion."

Kayla bit her lip at the sharp sting. As far as she was concerned, a man like him wasn't capable of love. He didn't care about Mercy or any of the girls he hurt. The lives he'd ruined. Because she'd seen them on the other side of that life. Girls who had been beaten with red-hot coat hangers to be kept in line, locked in hotel rooms and branded.

And now he wanted her to believe he was

somehow saving Mercy. That using things like voodoo to coerce her into working was just another day on the job. And that somehow he'd justified what he was doing and was under the illusion that she would want to come back to him.

"Here's your phone." He pulled the familiar cell from his pocket and held it up in front of her. "I want you to leave a voice message. Tell her you know she's in trouble, and to meet you at Amsterdam Central at noon."

Kayla stared at the phone. The railway station was the second busiest in the country. It was connected to both the national train system and the metro, which meant thousands of people passed through the place every day.

"And if she doesn't show up?"

"That's why it's up to you to convince her."

Kayla's mind scrambled for a way out. "And Levi and my father? If I do what you are asking, will you let them go?"

Betraying Mercy couldn't be an option. The only way out was to find a way to stop Mercy from showing up. Or to get to her first. But how?

"Are you ready? Because I won't hesitate to put a bullet through your or your boyfriend's head."

Her legs shook beneath her. She wanted

to tell him that he had it all wrong. That she wasn't in love with Levi. That she never had been. Never could be. That he didn't even matter to her. And yet if that were true...then why did her emotions seem in a tangled knot? But the reality was, it didn't matter how she felt. She didn't want anything to happen to him.

"Act natural," he said, dialing. "No games or you know what will happen."

The call went straight to voice mail.

"Mercy, this is Kayla." She drew in a short breath. "I'm sorry I missed lunch on Monday."

Nicu frowned, but she kept talking.

"Listen, I know you're in trouble and I want to help. Please. Meet me at Amsterdam Central today at noon. You should remember the station. We were there in November. I want to help."

Andrei stepped into the doorway and signaled at Nicu. They switched to another language, so she couldn't understand what they were talking about, but their body language and loud voices made it clear that something was wrong.

"What's going on?" she asked.

Nicu slipped her phone into his pocket, checked the cords binding her wrists and ankles, then secured a gag around her mouth. "I'm going out, but I won't be gone long. And in the meantime…don't do anything stupid."

The chilly hall was empty as Levi made his way down the corridor. He automatically reached for his phone, but his pocket was empty. Apparently they'd thought of everything, including making sure that he didn't have a way to communicate if he happened to escape. He shivered, wondering what had happened to his jacket. Not that it really mattered. The only thing he could think about at the moment was finding Kayla.

He kept his footsteps quiet as he moved down the hall. Shadows danced from some lanterns casting their flickering light against the wall. The only way he could ensure he found Kayla was to do a search of the house, room by room, until he found her. And that was going on the assumption that she was here. He opened a set of double doors. The wood floor creaked beneath him as he stepped into the large room. There was a piano in the corner, along with antique sofas that fit the architecture of the house. At one time the room must have been stunning. But from what he could tell, the place was now nothing more than a front for criminals.

He stepped back out into the hallway, wondering how an impulse decision to catch a flight to Europe had suddenly turned out to be so complicated. Especially when he was rarely impulsive. While he'd followed his brother to Amsterdam, he'd never imagined a scenario like this one. If only he were dealing with Adam right now, instead of a bunch of unnamed traffickers. But Adam had yet to answer his calls since Levi's arrival, and for the moment there were more serious issues to deal with than his little brother.

He fought to keep his focus as he continued searching the house, room by room, memorizing the floor plan as he went. While the potential of a stunning property was there, the house had clearly been neglected for years. From what he'd seen so far, there were at least two wings, two stories and dozens of rooms, most of which contained water marks on the ceiling and chipped, faded paint on the walls. But after thirty minutes, there was still no sign of Kayla or the men he'd heard earlier.

He stopped in front of three closed doors at the end of yet another narrow hallway. He opened the door of the first one and stepped into a bedroom that looked as if it hadn't been occupied for years. Layers of dust had settled across a walnut dresser and matching bed frame. A duvet lay on the bed, faded from years of sunlight, while cobwebs marked the ceiling. It was like the rest of the house. Empty and neglected.

So how had their abductors gotten their hands on the seemingly abandoned house? And what exactly were they using it for?

An image of the dead girl in the morgue filled his mind. An isolated place like this would be the perfect spot to temporarily hide girls who were being trafficked into the city and other locations. But if that was true, where were they? So far there was no sign of anyone living here. He had to keep looking.

The next door opened to yet another bedroom, but again, no sign of Kayla. He was getting frustrated. He'd been sure she was still with him when they'd pulled them out of the vehicle. Why would they have taken the time to move her somewhere else when they had this abandoned house?

No. She had to be here.

But even with his systematic search, there had to be something he was missing. Another wing, a basement or an attic. He stopped at the end of the hallway in front of a door that led outside to the back of the property, and he tried the handle. Every outside door and window he'd come across so far were securely locked with dead bolts that, as far as he was concerned, were impenetrable with his limited lock-picking skills.

Someone clearly didn't want him getting out.

Ten minutes later, he'd searched half a dozen more rooms, and there was still no sign of Kayla. No signs of a landline that would give him access to communicate with the outside world. Nothing.

I need to find her, God.

A flash of red caught his eye on the floor in the living room where he stood. He stopped and picked up the scarf Kayla had been wearing. He glanced around the room, the worry in his gut growing. She had been here, but where was she now? So far—besides the scarf—there had been no sign of Kayla. No sign of anyone.

He was running out of house and out of time. But if she wasn't here, where was she? He glanced back at the room filled with furniture from another era—couple of wing-back chairs, a long sofa and a few scattered paintings on the walls. Just because she'd been here didn't mean they hadn't taken her somewhere else. These men could potentially have property all across the city.

The thought sent a chill through him.

How many girls like Mercy had disappeared, never to be seen again until one day their lifeless bodies showed up at the morgue?

He heard a door slam and stopped.

Someone was definitely in the house.

Glancing around the room, he grabbed a poker from beside the fireplace and gripped it firmly in his hand. It might not be the best defense against a gun, but it would at least give him a chance. He started down a hallway he had yet to search, toward the sound of raised voices.

Another door slammed. Levi stopped. Footsteps ensued. Whoever was in the house was coming toward him.

He glanced down the hall. He needed to hide, but he also needed to see who they were. And if Kayla was with them. He grabbed the handle of the nearest door. Locked. The footsteps grew louder. He hurried to the next door, this time grateful it was unlocked. He stepped inside the room, leaving the door open a crack. Holding his breath, Levi prayed they weren't looking for him. If they realized he'd escaped, he could end up putting both his life and Kayla's in further danger.

The voices grew louder. Levi pressed his ear against the door and listened, straining to understand their conversation that sounded garbled to his ears. He heard them exit the house, then quickly moved to the window. He could see the sun peeking above the horizon. Seconds later, a car sped down the long driveway toward a wrought-iron gate. The vehicle was too far away for him to see clearly inside the car, but as far as he could tell, the two men had exited alone.

But why? Surely whoever had abducted them wouldn't have left them alone, unless they believed there was no chance of escape. One of the dogs barked in the distance, reminding him that they weren't exactly unattended. But if Kayla was in the house, he needed to find her. Because he had no doubt about one thing: they would be back.

With his senses on high alert, he resumed his search, starting with the locked door he'd passed. Most of the doors inside the house had been open, which made him wonder why they'd lock the door, unless there was something—or someone—they wanted to hide.

Levi quickly worked to pick the lock before stepping inside the room. Instead of old furniture, this space was a sparsely furnished office with a modern desk, a chair and a couple of metal file cabinets. He crossed the room, quickly searching the desk. Inside were folders and financial records. He glanced at the file cabinet, but as much as he'd like to know what was in that cabinet, his priority had to be finding Kayla. He made a mental note of the location, then continued down the hall.

Another dozen yards and two empty rooms later, the hallway dead-ended.

Levi turned around and jogged up a staircase to the second floor of the house, his pulse racing with frustration. He glanced out a window at the top of the stairs. There was no sign of the men returning, but his gut told him they'd be back soon. He needed to hurry.

The first door he came to was locked. He studied the lock, realizing immediately that this mechanism wasn't going to be easy to pick. He knocked on the door. The solid wood was going to be a disadvantage if he couldn't pick the lock. But if he was going to search the house properly, he needed to get into this room. A noise emanated from inside the room.

Kayla?

"Kayla, it's Levi. If that's you…"

He gave up on trying to pick the lock and decided instead to try plan B. With one swift motion, Levi drove the heel of his foot into the door. The wood splintered, so he did it a second time. If anyone else was in this house, he wasn't going to be able to keep his presence a secret, but at this point he didn't care. If he got caught, he'd deal with the situation, but in the meantime, he was going to find out if she was on the other side.

EIGHT

Kayla's gaze stayed fixed on the door as it slammed open, hitting the wall behind it.

A whoosh of air left her lungs as relief flooded through her. For a moment, she'd thought Nicu was back again. Instead, Levi stood towering over her like a knight in shining armor who'd just arrived to save the day. And with him here, they might actually be able to get out of here. Might be able to get to Mercy before Nicu found her.

"Hey…" He quickly tugged off the gag. "Sorry I took so long."

"Took so long?" She couldn't help but laugh. "I just can't believe you're here."

He knelt down in front of her and began working to untie her wrists. "Did they hurt you?"

"No." She glanced at the door, her heart still racing. If Nicu and his brother returned and caught them trying to escape… "But they will return."

"I know." He tugged at one of the knots with his teeth, then finally managed to loosen them.

Thirty seconds later, she was free.

She reached up and touched the side of his face. "You've got quite a shiner."

He wadded up the twine and tossed it into the corner of the room. "It's nothing. Trust me. I've had a lot worse."

"Thank you," she said. "For fighting for me."

He pointed to his eye. "Unfortunately I lost."

"Maybe, but I never stopped believing you'd find me. We don't have a lot of time. We've got to get out of here and find Mercy."

"So did you talk to them?" He started working on untying her feet.

She nodded. "One of them. They made me send Mercy a voice message, telling her to meet me at noon at the main train station. If I didn't, they assured me that we'd end up in the canal like the girl from the morgue."

"You did what you believed you had to do at that moment."

"Did I?" She'd yet to shake the guilt she felt. "My only plan was that we could somehow find her before they do. I'm also hoping she'll pick up on what I said between the lines and simply not show up."

"What do you mean?"

Kayla's mind replayed the message she'd left Mercy. "I told her I was sorry I missed lunch on Monday, which I didn't, and mentioned that we'd gone to the station last November, which we hadn't done, either."

"Smart girl," he said as the cords around her ankles finally came free. "Where is your phone?"

"They took it with them," she said as he helped her to her feet.

She glanced at the door again, wishing she could stop shaking. Wishing she didn't feel like crying.

"Kayla...hey...we're going to figure this out."

"I know. I'm just...scared. We've got to get to her before they do."

He hesitated, then pulled her against his chest. "We're going to find a way out of this, because there are no other options."

She nuzzled her face against his shoulder, wishing she wasn't acting like a blubbering baby. She'd always hated feeling out of control, but this was different. The stakes had risen, people's lives were on the line and she had no idea how to stop what was happening.

She took a step back and looked at him, sucking up as much courage as she could to replace the fear. "Is there a way out of this place?"

"Not that I've seen so far. Whoever's behind this clearly doesn't want us to leave. And while I haven't searched the entire house, all the doors to the outside that I've come across are bolted shut. I did see a couple of windows we might be able to get through, though most of them are barred. And then, once we're outside the house, there are guard dogs and a large fence surrounding at least part of the property."

A piece of cake. Right.

She glanced out the window overlooking the front drive and the neglected tree-studded yard and felt the panic returning.

How in the world are we supposed to get out of here, God?

"So do you have any idea where we are?" she asked.

"No, though we have to be out of the city, and from what I've been able to see, the property around this house is huge."

The walls of the room pressed in around her, pushing her toward a full-blown panic attack. "There has to be a way out of here. We've got to get out before they return."

"I know." He brushed his fingers across her arm. "But I don't think we can go yet."

She caught his gaze and realized what he was thinking. "You think my father might be here."

"I do."

She prayed he was right, but the reminder of her father brought another wave of guilt. What if he wasn't here? What if they didn't find him? She'd invited him to come stay with her in order to take care of him, and now his life was in danger because of her.

"When I was looking for you," Levi continued, "I searched a large section of the house. It's huge, easily ten to fifteen thousand square feet, which means we need to keep looking. And on top of that, I found an office downstairs. There could be evidence that could give us leverage we need in getting back not only Mercy, but your father as well if we don't find him here."

Kayla nodded but couldn't help noting the risks. They didn't know if her father was here, but she knew without a doubt that if Nicu and his brother came back and caught them, things were not going to end well. But this might very well be their only chance to find him.

"Ok. Let's go."

Maybe they could find both her father and Mercy before it was too late.

"We won't stay longer than we have to, but we still need to search the rest of this wing," Levi said, heading out the door. "And while we search for your father, we'll look for a way out."

She rubbed the backs of her wrists where the cords had rubbed against her skin as she followed him out of the room. Her entire body ached. She was thirsty and hungry, but none of that mattered at the moment.

"What kind of leverage are you hoping to find?" she asked.

"Anything thing that might tell us who these people are, including finances or some kind of paper trail that would prove they're holding girls against their will and forcing them to work as prostitutes."

Which in turn might make a way for them to save both her father and Mercy.

Kayla followed him down the long hallway, queasy from worry and exhaustion. Black-and-white portraits hung on vintage gold, textured wallpaper. Antique wall sconces helped light the otherwise darkened hallway. On any other day, she would have loved the chance to explore the old house. But not today. Not now. Every second that passed meant a second closer to their abductors' return.

"Is there anything else you can tell me about the men?" Levi asked as he opened the next door that led to another bedroom.

She drew in a slow breath before answering. "The one who spoke with me was Nicu, the man Ana mentioned. The second man was Andrei, who has to be his brother. They both sounded like they were from eastern Europe."

"And what did they want besides for you to call Mercy?"

"Apparently he's convinced I know where Mercy is and he decided that kidnapping my father wasn't enough motivation. They have pictures of us outside the morgue and accused us of going to the police. And the girl we saw at the morgue…" A shiver ran through her. "He told me she was one of theirs. Another stab at motivating me to give him Mercy."

"I'm so sorry." He stopped in front of her then rubbed his hands up and down her arms. "You're freezing."

"I'll be okay."

Except it wasn't the temperature outside or the dampness inside that had her shivering.

"When you were looking for me, did you see any signs that people were living here?"

Levi started walking again, and she hurried to keep up with him. "No."

"Like you said, though, this is the perfect location. It's off the grid, and the dense vegetation and hedges surrounding the property keep it private. Who would think about a bunch of girls locked up in a place like this?"

"Unfortunately, all I saw was some food in the kitchen fridge. Nothing else." Levi opened the next closed door and took a step inside the empty room. There was still no sign of her father. "Back to Nicu and his brother... Do you know why they left?"

"I think maybe they got a phone call. Andrei was clearly angry. The two of them started fighting. And while I'm not sure what it is, there's something else I noticed. There is something personal about all of this. Nicu's relationship with Mercy. I got the impression it's not just about money."

"What do you mean?" Levi stopped in front of the next open door, which led into a library with eight-foot bookshelves. "Are you saying he loves her?"

"I don't know. Maybe. In his own twisted way."

"Even someone like Nicu has to have a

weakness. You said they were fighting. Do you know what they were fighting about?"

"No. They weren't speaking English." She quickly scanned the room, feeling the urgency to find her father and get out. "But Andrei was clearly upset, and whatever he said upset Nicu as well. It was obvious Nicu didn't want to leave, but he checked my wrists to make sure I wasn't going anywhere, and that was the last time I saw him."

The wind had picked up outside, its eerie howling growing louder as they reached the end of the wing, where there was a large sunroom filled with an assortment of wicker chairs and small tables.

Levi stepped up to one of the windows that was secured with an iron bar and let out a sharp sigh. Below them, the overgrown property with its tangled brush and trees stretched out as far as she could see. To the east was a tennis court next to an outdoor building. From this vantage point, she could see the opposite wing of the house, its brick exterior covered with ivy.

She glanced back at the tennis court. It was possible there were more buildings on the large plot. A garage or maybe a shed. From what she could tell, the property covered several acres. How in the world were they going to search the entire plot? But if her father wasn't in the house, he had to be out there somewhere.

"We need to keep moving," Levi said, pulling her out of her thoughts.

"Where else is there to look?" Kayla followed Levi back down a staircase.

"There are still a few more rooms down the other side of this hall and then the office downstairs. Then after that, I don't think we have any options other than to try to leave."

"Levi, wait..." She grabbed his arm, unwilling to give up. "My father has to be here somewhere. Where else would they have taken him? There could be other buildings on this property."

"I know." But it could take hours to search the property, and he was pretty sure they didn't have hours.

"If we don't find my father soon—" she tried unsuccessfully to hide the panic in her voice "—they will kill him."

Levi hurried down the hall toward the next door, uncertain how wise it would be to search the entire property. On foot, a search would be tedious, and that didn't even begin to take into consideration the guard dogs waiting for them as soon as they found a way out of the house. But they'd have to deal with that problem once they found a way out.

Something creaked on the other side of the hall. He glanced down the passageway. In an old house like this, noises could come from anywhere—expanding ductwork, rodents, water heaters or pipes. But still, they couldn't be too cautious.

He started walking again. Maybe he'd just imagined the noise.

"Levi...what is it?"

He glanced at Kayla, not wanting to worry her any more than she already was, as he opened another door. "I thought I heard something."

She followed his gaze down the hallway behind them.

"I'm sure it's nothing," he said. "This place is old."

He could see the fear mixed with disappointment in her eyes. Fear from the situation they were in. Disappointment from not finding Max. He easily could have missed a section of the house, a basement or, for that matter, even a hidden room. From his earlier search he knew that the two-story house had a kitchen, a bar, a library, half a dozen or more bedroom suites, plus a small reception hall. Plenty of spaces to hide.

He shut the door behind him and turned to her. "Anything?"

She shook her head. "Just a few pieces of furniture. Nothing personal at all."

"We need to get out of here, but let's look through their office first. Five minutes, tops."

He trod softly against the tiled floors, listening for any noises, while they started down a narrow, winding staircase. He'd been impressed by the way she'd dealt with the past twenty-four hours, because he knew it hadn't been easy. It was clear she'd invested herself completely in her job, in women like Mercy and the others who she dealt with on a day-to-day basis. She'd do anything in her power to keep them safe.

Now it was up to him to keep her safe.

Inside the office, he started going through the desk drawers, trying to find some clue as to who was behind this, but so far nothing stood out.

He glanced at one of the file cabinets. He needed to get inside.

"I didn't know they taught you to pick locks in the army," she said as he started working on the lock.

He looked up at her unapologetically. "Let's just say that you never know when covert-entry training might come in handy."

He started pulling out file folders and setting them on the desk.

"What have you got?" Kayla asked, stepping up next to him.

"I'm not sure exactly, but it looks to me like it could be some sort of a financial paper trail."

Kayla opened up one of the files and glanced at the stamp at the top of one of the papers. "This word, *inzet*, means 'auction.' I used to go to them in the States all the time and have gone a couple times here. It's definitely possible to purchase a house far below market value this way."

"So they bought this property in an auction?"

"About six weeks ago, it looks like," she said, moving back to the file cabinet. "But it makes sense. Like any big business, they need banks and property in order to operate."

"So if they're not already, they have to be planning to use this house for the girls."

"What's that?" she asked, turning around toward the door.

Levi's attention shifted toward the hallway. He'd heard something, too.

"Someone's out there," she said, glancing at the door.

"If they're back, it's not going to take them long to find us."

He stared toward the hallway. They should have run when they had the chance. A dog started barking. Something must have alerted them.

He heard a door slam.

"Do you think they're back?" Kayla asked.

"I didn't hear a car drive up, but someone's in the house. We need to get out of here."

Another door opened and closed.

A chill swept over her. "Someone's doing a systematic search."

Whoever was here had to know they'd managed to escape.

"And my father, or the girls? If they're here somewhere?"

"We'll send the police back, but we can't do anything if we're tied up."

He glanced at the files he'd just found and wondered if they were risking giving Nicu time to destroy the evidence if they ran. Staying wasn't a risk he was willing to take, but they could bring the evidence with them.

He grabbed a small backpack from the floor, quickly dumped out the contents and began filling it with the financial papers and files.

"You said all the outside doors were bolted shut," she said.

"They are, but there was one bathroom window with no bars. I think we should be able to crawl through it."

He stepped out into the hallway with the backpack over his shoulder and the fire poker he'd been carrying this entire time, pausing only for a moment to orient himself to where he'd seen the bathroom.

"Are you sure you can find it?" Kayla asked.

"Yes. It was on the main floor, on the other side of the house where they had me locked up."

They walked through a large living area he'd passed through while looking for her. While most of the rooms looked neglected, this one retained some of its former glory with heavy gold drapes on the windows along with an eclectic mixture of antique furniture. But it wasn't the decor that held his attention. He heard another door shut. Whoever was in the house was getting closer.

He signaled at Kayla to head toward the bathroom ahead of him. He'd almost lost her once. He wasn't going to let that happen again.

NINE

Kayla stepped into the tiled bathroom in front of Levi, who quickly locked the door behind them. She glanced at the square window on the opposite side of the room. He was right. It would be tight, but there were no bars, and they should be able to get through it. What she wasn't sure of was if there was enough time to get out before they got caught.

"It's going to be hard to cover up the sound of breaking glass," she said, opening up the cupboards under the sink to search for a towel that would help muffle the noise.

Levi eyed the window. "True, but we can either try to escape this way, or play cat and mouse until Nicu and his brother return, which would greatly lessen our odds of getting out. I just don't know how I missed whoever's out there while I was searching the house."

She tried not to think about the possibility

they were leaving her father behind. Levi had been right when he said there was no way to know if he was somewhere on the property. And that they couldn't help him if they were both locked up as well. But that didn't stop the worry over what might have happened to him from gnawing at her gut.

I'm trying to trust You, God, but there is so much at stake here.

Trying to focus, she pulled some thick towels from one of the shelves beneath the sink. "It doesn't matter now what we missed. We just need to get out of here."

"I figure we've got a couple minutes, tops, before they figure out where we are and they find a way in." Levi climbed up on the counter that ran beneath the window.

He hadn't mentioned it, but she knew what he had to be thinking. Despite strict gun laws in the Netherlands, Nicu and his brother had both been armed. Which meant whoever was outside that door was probably armed as well. A face-to-face encounter would be risky and something they wanted to avoid.

She glanced at the door. She hadn't heard any more noises outside the bathroom, but that didn't mean that whoever was out there wasn't getting closer. How had they gotten to this point where they were being forced to run for their lives?

Her mind shifted to her sister, Lilly, which brought with it a familiar panic. A spiraling chain of events had taken a straight-A high school student and thrust her into the dark world of human trafficking. All it had taken was a string of bad decisions and one person who'd taken advantage of her naivety, and she'd lost her sister forever. And now another frightening chain of events had brought her here. She couldn't lose her father as well. He was all she had left.

"Kayla?"

"Sorry." Her chest heaved as she handed him one of the towels. She had to stay focused, because the men who'd taken them played by an entirely different moral code. The only way to save her father was to get out of this house and go for help.

"Just be careful," she said.

Levi steadied himself on the counter, then jabbed at the window with the end of the fire poker a couple of times. As soon as the glass shattered, he quickly ran the poker around the edges of the window to finish breaking out the rest of the glass.

"Give me the towel and the glass," she said. She carefully dumped both the towel and the shards into the bathtub, then handed him the second towel to lay over the window frame and protect them from getting cut. Another door shut. Apparently, whoever was out there had every intention of searching the entire house room by room until they found them.

"I want you to go first." Levi held out his hand to help hoist her up on the counter. "Just wait for me on the other side. I'll be right behind you."

She took his hand, then froze. The handle of the door rattled behind them, followed by someone trying to kick in the door. The door buckled slightly, and the lock held, but it wouldn't for long. Kayla caught Levi's gaze. They'd just run out of time. There was no way both of them could get out of the house before whoever was on the other side of the door broke through.

Levi jumped down from the counter, motioning her toward the corner on the other side of the door.

"What are you going to do?"

"Hit them with the element of surprise." Levi held up the fire poker and positioned himself in front of the door. "I'm going to have about half a second to disarm whoever walks through that door."

The third time, the frame split and the door burst open.

Levi lunged forward in one sweeping motion, taking the tall blond man by surprise as he slammed the fire poker against the man's hand that was holding a gun. Before the man could recover, Levi struck again, this time swinging the fire poker behind his knees and dropping him to the ground. But neither man had any intention of going down without a fight. The man quickly stumbled back onto his feet and swung the gun, hitting Levi across the side of his face.

The two scrimmaged until Levi managed to slam the man against the wall, face-first, and pulled back the arm that held the gun. The man cried out in pain, then dropped the gun.

The weapon skidded across the tiled floor. Hands shaking, Kayla took a step forward and grabbed the gun, then aimed it at their attacker. The man stumbled backward, giving Levi an opening for one more solid punch. A second later, their attacker was out cold on the white tiles.

"Are you okay?" She knelt down next to Levi, who was still breathing hard from the fight, and handed him the weapon. "I know that had to hurt."

"It's just a few nasty bruises." He shot her a half smile. "What about you?"

"I'll be okay."

He didn't need to know that everything about today terrified her. Or that her heart wouldn't stop racing. But who in her place wouldn't feel the same way she did right now?

"We need to tie him up before he wakes up," Levi said. "Help me take off his coat and his boots. We can use the laces to secure his hands and feet."

A phone clattered out of the man's pocket as Levi shifted his leg.

"Wait a minute… This is my phone." She picked it up, noting the crack across the screen.

The man groaned.

Kayla shoved the phone into her pocket and went back to undoing the laces, hurrying to finish before he woke up. "Why would he have my phone?"

"Good question. Nicu must have given it to him." Levi finished securing the man's hands with the laces, then nudged him awake. "Get up."

Pointing the gun at the small of his back, Levi managed to get him back into the living room, then tied his feet to a chair as an extra precaution.

Frowning, Levi stepped in front of the guard and grabbed a ring of keys from the other man's belt. "I think it's time you answered a few questions."

Levi crouched next to the guard, knowing full well that not only did they need information, they needed it quickly. Three deployments in the Middle East had taught him patience when it came to interviewing suspects. His job had been not only to fight terrorist threats, but to neutralize foreign intelligence, which meant gaining trust, conducting security investigations and processing evidence. And just like today, the circumstances were never perfect.

But right now they didn't have the luxury of time on their side. He had little to no leverage, let alone solid information that went beyond a pile of files. Nothing that solidified his upper hand and would force the man to give them what they wanted. He couldn't threaten him with jail time, and there were no deals that could be made to motivate him to talk. But somehow he had to convince the man—before Nicu and his brother returned—that confessing was the best thing to do. Which meant time was working against them.

"Who are you?" Levi asked, stepping in front of the guard.

The man turned his head away, as if he were totally uninterested.

"Do you speak English?"

No response.

Kayla grabbed her phone and pulled up a photo of her father. "Maybe he has something to say about this."

"Do you recognize him?" he asked.

The guard stared at the ground, still ignoring them.

"What about her?" Kayla asked, flipping to a photo of Mercy.

"That's okay," Levi continued. "All you have to do right now is listen. We know that your boss—I'm going to assume Nicu is your boss—is involved in the trafficking of young girls from across Eastern Europe, Africa and Asia."

"And even if you're not involved in the actual trafficking of these young girls," Kayla added, "there are stiff laws that include those aiding the smugglers."

"Why don't you elaborate on what kind of sentences we're looking at," Levi said, nodding at Kayla. "What kind of future does he have to look forward to?"

"A maximum sentence of twelve years for

a single offense, fifteen if the victim of the crime is a minor. And aggravated human trafficking—which includes recruiting, harboring or transporting someone under the age of eighteen—can mean life in prison."

"And this girl," Levi said, tapping on the photo of Mercy, "this girl is only seventeen years old."

The guard looked up and caught Levi's gaze, but this time the earlier confidence he'd noted was gone. "You found a few papers, so what? You don't know anything."

Levi took a step back. "So you do speak English. Good. I'll ask you again. Who are you? And by the way, you'd be surprised at how much we do know."

The man's lips furrowed into a deeper frown. "Yes, I work here for Nicu, but that doesn't mean I'm involved in what he's doing. I'm just the guard."

Levi glanced toward the window and the front driveway and held up the ring of keys he'd procured from the guard's belt loop. "I have a feeling that Nicu and his buddy aren't going to be too thrilled when they show up and discover you've allowed us to escape."

"Except you haven't escaped. Not yet. The moment I realized the two of you had gotten out of your rooms, I called them. They're on their way back to the house now and will be here any minute."

Levi glanced at a clock hanging on the wall. If the guard was telling the truth, they were taking a huge risk staying here.

"And on top of that," the guard continued, "you might have the keys to the front door, but try getting past those guard dogs. They're highly trained attack dogs that will be happy to eat you for lunch."

Levi kept his own expression neutral, wishing he could ignore the fact that the man might be right. "We'll see about that, but before we leave, I need to know who else is in this house."

"Beside the three of us?" The guard shrugged, clearly trying to play hardball. "No one."

"What about the girls they bring through?" Kayla asked. "What about my father?"

"Who Nicu brings to his house is his business. I was hired simply to run security. Especially when we have guests."

"How many *guests* come through this lovely estate?" Levi asked.

"Not many. Nicu's a private person. He prefers the quiet of the countryside."

"Which would explain the huge estate in the middle of nowhere. And the fact that he's kidnapped a least three Americans in the past twenty-four hours."

Levi caught the flicker of alarm in the guard's eyes. He might claim to be ignorant, but the man knew far more than he was letting on.

"Here's the bottom line," Levi said. "We know your boss is a part of a human trafficking ring. And we're pretty sure that they bring them here before they end up on the streets."

His gaze shifted. "This estate is nothing more than an investment bought by my boss. You watch those American shows where they flip houses, don't you? You can make a ton of money on a place like this bought at auction. Nicu's planning to double his money this time around."

"A real estate flipper. That's interesting. Because from what I've seen on these American shows, most of the time those real estate investors don't kidnap people on the side."

"Nicu doesn't like it when people try to get into his business."

"Maybe, but I have a feeling that Nicu isn't going to be happy when he finds you tied to a chair after you let us go. But that's fine. Because we know what's really been going on here and plan to make sure the police know as well."

"Forget it. You can't pin anything on me."

"Not even murder?" Kayla asked.

"Murder? What are you talking about?"

Levi glanced at Kayla. Maybe she'd found a nerve to strike after all. Maybe their guard drew the line at murder.

"The body of a young girl was dredged out of the canal yesterday," Kayla said. "One of Nicu's girls. Apparently that's what he does to people who cross him."

"Like I said, you have nothing on me."

"You're wrong," she said, clearly not finished. "We're gathering evidence that can put you behind bars for the rest of your life, and I promise I will do everything in my power to ensure that is what happens. And not just for the unlawful trafficking of these girls, but for the kidnapping of my father as well."

"Like I said, you've got nothing."

The guard simply shook his head and laughed. They weren't getting anywhere.

"You think this is amusing?" she asked. "Because you won't when you're sitting in a jail cell. Tell me where my father is."

"Lady, I don't have to tell you anything.

So if you think that your threats are going to work, forget it."

Levi glanced at Kayla. Without more time, he doubted there was anything else he could get out of the man. And he wasn't willing to risk running into Nicu.

Levi pulled Kayla aside. "It's over. We need to go. Now."

"Not yet. He's lying. He has to know where my father is."

"He's not going to tell us, Kayla. He's just going to try to keep stalling us. That's what he wants. Because he is right about one thing. Nicu will return, and if we're still standing here playing bad cop, good cop when he does, we're not going to be able to do anything to help your father."

Her jaw quivered. "If he's here and we leave, you know what they'll do to him."

"We'll find a way to put an end to all of this, but this isn't the way. Not anymore. We need to leave so we can help your father."

He could read the conflict in her eyes. The deep frustration and feelings of helplessness that made him wish desperately he could fix this. But if they stayed any longer, they could easily forfeit any chance of finding her father altogether.

"Kayla…we need to go."

She nodded. "I know."

"I'm sorry," he said, pulling on the guard's jacket.

She pressed her lips together and grabbed the backpack. "Let's go."

TEN

Kayla waited while Levi unlocked the front door with the guard's key, praying that after making it this far, they'd find a way off the property.

"You okay?" he asked, slipping the set of keys into his pocket.

"I will be once we get out of here."

She blinked back the tears, overwhelmed by the enormity of the situation. They might be out of the house, but they weren't exactly home free. She glanced down the long walk that led to the driveway and studied the terrain. The house rested on the south side of the property. The surrounding vegetation and green lawn—dense like the gardens around them—were big enough that she couldn't see the edges of the property. Which meant all they had to do now was make it to the wall, scale the perimeter fence, then find a ride back into the city without getting caught.

Right.

"Where are the dogs?" she asked, wrapping the scarf Levi had found around her neck to block the wind. The sun might be up, but the temperatures had yet to rise.

"I don't know, but I saw two of them from the house. German shepherds."

"Ready to eat us for lunch," she mumbled.

"Are you afraid of dogs?" he asked as they headed away from the house toward the front gate, keeping close to the overgrown tree line as they went.

"I love them, actually. But that doesn't mean I'm in the mood for an encounter with a couple of attack dogs."

She stuffed her hands into her pockets in an attempt to ward off the cold and felt her phone. She pulled it out and went to her contact list. Her first priority had to be finding a way to get a hold of Mercy in order to ensure she didn't show up at the train station.

"Kayla, wait." Levi wrapped his hand around her fingers that were holding the phone.

"What's wrong? We can make sure Mercy doesn't show up at Amsterdam Central."

"Which would be great, but before we try to call Mercy or the cavalry, we need to make sure Nicu isn't tracking the phone's GPS or monitoring its calls."

"In case Mercy tries to call me." She sobered at the words.

He nodded. "We can't take a chance of us leading them to her."

She let him take the phone. "You think they what...put some sort of spyware on my phone?"

"Since we found that one guy with spy gear at the girls' apartment? Yeah. I'm not putting anything past them. Not at this point. Who knows what his plan is?" He nodded toward the house. "I know we need to get out of here, but this shouldn't take long. Just keep an eye out for the dogs."

She glanced back toward the house while Levi went to work on the phone—and she battled the sick feeling growing inside her. They were standing beneath a copse of trees that should keep them hidden if Nicu drove up, but as much as they needed a phone to call for help, they also needed to get off the property.

"How did you learn all of this?" she asked, clueless as to what was involved in detecting spyware.

"It helps if you run a company with a highly qualified security officer who insists on training that goes beyond private board meetings and occasional security emails. He thought it might come in handy one day after a handful of threats, so I spent a couple days with our IT guys. They taught me a ton of stuff."

"Regarding security threats?"

"That's where it started. About six months ago, instead of getting a new phone, I decided to get mine fixed at a local repair shop. But after I got it back, I noticed that my data usage had increased significantly and there were often strange background noises when I made a call."

"All from spyware?"

"A disgruntled employee had paid off someone to put the malware on my phone in an attempt to gain some inside trading information." He shook his head. "Looks like the GPS was turned off, probably in case the police try and track it, but I also found spyware."

So Levi had been right.

"There's a trap door in this particular spyware that will monitor any calls. Getting rid of it is going to be tricky. I'm going to have to find and delete those files."

She was pacing again, both from nerves and trying to stay warm. Another roadblock wasn't what they needed right now.

"Is this worth waiting for?" she asked.

"It is if we're going to try to get help."

The sound of a motor in the distance caught her attention. Sun reflected off a vehicle as it drove through the front gate and started up the drive. Nicu—or someone—was here.

Levi grabbed her hand. "I've started running an update that should delete the spyware. But in the meantime, we need to get out of here."

He didn't have to tell her twice.

They ran east, away from the driveway, careful to stay among the overgrown trees and bushes. But keeping hidden wasn't going to be enough. Levi had seen the dogs, and they also knew that at least the front part of the property was fenced, if not the entire property. They had to find a way out and to the main road before Nicu realized they weren't in the house and came searching for them.

Which meant at this point, every second counted.

Kayla held her breath as a black sedan with tinted windows in the back drove past them, its tires crunching the gravel beneath it. She stifled a sneeze as the vehicle finally stopped at the end of the drive, then Nicu and his brother jumped out and headed for the house.

"It's them," she said.

"Let's go."

Levi took her hand again and headed toward the front gate, careful to stay in the shadows. Praying desperately that they weren't seen.

"How much time do you think we have until they start searching outside the house?" she asked.

"I'm guessing just as long as it takes to meet up with the security guard and get his side of the story."

Which meant minutes at the most.

A ten-foot iron fence topped with razor wire surrounded the property as far as she could see. Getting over it was going to be difficult if not impossible. They started along the perimeter of the fence toward the front gate, searching for a way out.

"I'm not seeing an easy way over this fence," she said.

"I agree, and the property's too big for us to take the time to check out the entire fence line for vulnerabilities."

"We could head for the front gate," Kayla said. "It should be possible to open it manually."

Levi glanced at her. "So in other words, we need to hope it's easier to get out than in."

"Exactly."

And if Nicu and his brother started searching the grounds before they got out of here…

He was still holding her hand as they slipped through the trees toward the gate. It wasn't the first time she realized how thankful she was that he was here. There was something protective about his presence. Something that managed to quiet her anxious spirit. For a moment, she couldn't help but wonder what it would be like to let him wrap his arms around her and promise her that nothing was going to hurt her. Not the dogs. Not Nicu or his security detail.

But that was a place she couldn't go.

Show us what to do, God…

Because there were no guarantees that he was going to be able to get them out of here without getting caught. And her falling apart wasn't going to help, either.

She kept moving alongside Levi, alert for any signs of either the dogs or Nicu. Levi squeezed her hand tighter as they ran, giving her a shot of courage that worked to calm her nerves.

Kayla stumbled over a fallen branch, then quickly regained her balance. Movement caught the corner of her eye and she momentarily slowed down. The two German shepherds were running toward them.

"Levi, forget Nicu…we've got a second problem."

Levi heard the dogs a split second before he saw them.

"Kayla…we need to run—"

"Stop. Stay where you are." She let go of his hand, then tugged gently on the sleeve of his jacket. "We need to stay still and calm. Avoid any eye contact and don't turn your back on the dogs."

Her command threw him off. He was used to making split-second decisions—and right now his assessment of the situation said run—but something about the urgency in her voice made him follow her lead.

"Do you really think that's a good strategy at this point?" he asked.

"You might be the expert on military stuff, but my grandfather used to train K-9 handlers. Which is why I know dogs and that running at this point is worse."

"I'd forgotten about that," he said, still not totally convinced.

But there was no way they could get back to

the house or, for that matter, to the perimeter fence, before the dogs caught up with them.

"Gramps taught me everything I know. Most dogs aren't planning to bite, even when they're aggressive. Well-trained attack dogs don't attack unless their owners are being threatened or they've been given a command. But if you run, they're going to instinctively chase us, and if that happens, they will catch us."

"Not if we can run faster than the dogs."

"Trust me, the odds are against that happening. It will amp up their aggression, and we will lose. I've seen it happen more than once. So no sudden arm movements, hands in your pockets, no eye contact."

Levi felt his blood pressure go up. He'd faced human enemies with less apprehension than this. "These aren't family pets, Kayla. They're trained guard dogs."

They were now thirty yards away and closing in quickly.

"I know," she said.

"We've got less than ten seconds until they're here. Are you sure about this?"

"Face them, but don't make eye contact. Hopefully if we stay still they will calm down and lose interest."

Hopefully?

He didn't like those odds.

But while he still wasn't convinced, he was going to trust her on this one. "Did I ever tell you that I was bitten by a dog when I was seven? I still have a scar from the encounter."

"Did you run?"

He frowned. "Touché."

Five more seconds.

He'd run, and the dog had bitten into the side of his calf. Since then he'd never felt comfortable around large dogs.

"Just don't move, Levi."

The dogs were close enough now that he could see their teeth and the muscles rippling beneath their fur. Which meant despite her confidence, every muscle in his own body was still screaming at him to run.

He studied the dogs without making eye contact. They slowed their pace as they approached them, intense with each step forward, teeth bared. That couldn't be a good sign.

"What do I do if they decide to attack?" he whispered.

"Try to put something between you and the dog."

Like what? My arm?

"If they do happen to knock you down," she

continued, "roll into a ball and lie still, covering your head and face with your hands."

Right.

"What if your plan doesn't work?" he asked.

He could hear Kayla's steady breathing next to him as she appeared to be studying the dogs' reactions. The animals seemed confused. Like they were ready for a chase, but no one was running. Maybe she'd been right after all.

He let out a puff of air. "Kayla…"

"Zitten."

He caught the calm authority in her voice and prayed her plan would work. Because there was going to be no second chances.

"Zitten," she repeated.

The dogs sat.

"You told them to sit?"

"Yes."

"So we've got dogs that speak Dutch," he mumbled, still not moving a muscle.

"What did you expect them to speak?"

"I don't know. I didn't exactly think about language skills while imagining being strewn across the yard in pieces by this point."

"You do have a point."

"We need to get to the gate." He turned slightly in order to eye the fence, but they were still at least twenty yards away. "How do you want us to do this without turning away from the dogs?"

"Start walking back slowly toward the gate."

Her plan might have worked so far, but what was going to happen when they started moving? They couldn't simply stand here forever. And if Nicu and his brother showed up in the meantime and gave commands to attack them, any impasse happening at the moment was going to be over.

"I'm going to start moving toward the gate," he said.

"Okay. Just move slowly."

He didn't need a reminder. He started backing up, freezing for a moment when a dry branch cracked beneath his foot.

"Keep moving," she said.

Another fifteen yards…ten…

His heart was still racing, and they were running out of time. He hadn't come all this way to keep her safe to have them mauled by a couple of guard dogs. He took another step backward, staying parallel with Kayla as she spoke to the dogs in a soft, soothing voice. The dogs were still sitting, though he could see their muscles tensing through their thick coats. He had no idea how much time they had.

"I'm going to have to try to open the gate manually," he said.

"No quick moves," she said. "Just slow and steady."

He turned slightly, continuing his earlier prayer for protection, then searched for the manual release. Finally finding it, he pulled it out, then grabbed the iron bars of the gate. They moved an inch. He let out a sharp sigh of relief.

"You need to come closer to the gate," he said.

Kayla nodded then began moving toward him.

She continued to talk to them with each step. The dogs were following her but showed no sign of aggression. Somehow, he needed to get the two of them out of the gate while ensuring that the dogs stayed on the inside.

He opened the gate a few more inches, just enough to allow them to escape. "Go."

She slipped through the opening in front of him. A second later, he was outside the property beside her. He quickly slid the gate back into place.

"You okay?" he asked.

She stared back at the dogs. "My heart's

racing like a jackhammer, and I'm ready for all of this to be over, but I think so."

"I've obviously discovered a new talent of yours. I think I might have to start calling you the dog whisperer. You were incredible."

She pulled her gloves out of her pockets and tugged them on. "I guess summers with my grandfather paid off."

He hadn't remembered that about her. Along with so many other things he wanted to know.

But not now.

Right now, they needed to get as far away from this property as possible.

Someone shouted from the house. He turned toward the commotion. Nicu was calling the dogs, who were now running toward the house. If they'd found the guard—which he was sure they had—then they knew he and Kayla had escaped and would come looking for them.

"We need to get out of here now."

They started sprinting away from the property with no idea which direction they should be going. The dogs were barking in the background, making him grateful—not for the first time—that they were on the other side of the fence. He just hoped that they hadn't missed anything inside the house. If Max was somewhere on the property, Levi's gut told him Nicu wouldn't hesitate to kill him.

But there was nothing he could do at this point. His priority had to be to get Kayla to safety. Which meant they needed to keep moving.

Levi glanced down the road. Along the front of the property ran a thick row of trees and brush, but less than a half a mile ahead of them, from what he could see from here, the terrain opened up. Which meant it would be harder to stay hidden. And while Nicu might be searching the property right now, it was only going to be a matter of time before he and his brother realized they'd managed to escape through the gate.

Grabbing Kayla's hand, he slowed his pace slightly but kept them moving. "We need a way out of here."

"I could call someone from work, but it would take too long for them to get here."

"Agreed, but there doesn't seem like a lot of traffic out here."

Which was an understatement. In the ten minutes or so that they'd been out here, he'd noted only one passing vehicle.

"Do you have any idea where we are?" he asked, as the house where they'd been held started to disappear from sight.

"I've spent time cycling the countryside with a couple friends, but nothing looks familiar. Which doesn't surprise me. Holland is covered with a network of bike routes and open terrain like this."

Which meant all he knew to do for now was to keep moving away from the property and pray that a car would come along and take them back to the city.

A minute later, Kayla tugged on his hand. "Levi…there's a car coming."

He let out a sharp sigh of relief, but his relief was quickly overshadowed by a wave of alarm as Kayla headed for the road. A small sports car was driving their direction, but that wasn't what had him apprehensive. A black vehicle had just turned onto the road behind the sports car. The black sedan Nicu had been driving.

ELEVEN

Kayla rushed out from the cover of the brush toward the road at the sight of the sports car driving toward them. Relief washed through her. From what she'd heard, hitchhiking wasn't as popular as it once was, but hopefully whoever was driving the car coming toward them would feel sorry for them and offer them a ride back to the city.

She stepped closer to the road.

"Kayla, stop! That's Nicu's vehicle behind them."

"What?"

Levi pulled her back into the shadows of the overgrown brush. She dropped down onto the ground and lay still beside him. The only movement was her heart pounding at the fatal mistake she'd almost made.

But had Nicu seen them? There was no way at this point to know for sure.

Her lungs felt as if they were about to burst.

She'd known they'd come looking for them. She should have been more careful. Because if they *had* seen her and Levi...

She watched the silver Porsche drive past. The knot in her stomach tightened. Nicu's car slowed down as it came closer to them.

Please, God...don't let him see us.

Kayla pressed her hands into the ground as the car passed where they were crouched in the dirt. She could see Nicu look intently into the brush where they lay, but he didn't stop. Maybe he hadn't seen them.

"How in the world are we supposed to get out of here?" she whispered.

"I don't know."

She watched as the sedan continued down the road until it was almost out of sight. "You think they're heading back to the city?"

"Not yet. I think he's still looking for us."

She knew he was right. Nicu was driving too slowly. Searching the terrain for a sign of them. She was still afraid to move. If they found her, they'd do more than simply ask her a bunch of questions this time.

Her cell rang in her pocket. She fumbled for the phone, regretting not putting it on vibrate. But Nicu's car just kept moving forward.

She checked out the caller ID before quickly turning down the sound.

The number was blocked.

"Are you sure he can't track us or monitor this call?" she asked.

"If they could track us, they would have already found us." Levi glanced at the phone. "You think it's him?"

The phone was still ringing.

She drew in a deep breath, nodded, then answered the phone and put it on speaker.

"Don't think this is over or that you've won." She immediately recognized Nicu's voice.

"What do you want?"

"Bottom line? I believe you don't know where Mercy is, but I also believe you can find her. Which means our old deal is back in play."

"We never had a deal. You kidnapped my father and now are trying to use him as leverage."

"Just listen carefully. I'm giving you twenty-four more hours to find her. I'll send you a text at this time tomorrow morning, telling you where we will meet."

She glanced at Levi, wondering when this was going to be over.

"If you keep your end of the deal," Nicu continued, "I'll let your father go. But if you go to the police or get anyone else involved,

I promise you'll never see your father again. And, Kayla…don't forget the girl in the morgue. I'm not in the mood to play games. You might have managed to get away this time, but if you don't do what I've told you, I will not only kill your father, but I will find you. And I will kill you, too."

The call dropped.

Kayla's hands shook. The vehicle turned around in the distance, then drove past them a second time.

"We need to keep moving," Levi said once the car had faded into the distance.

"Once we get to the end of this grove of trees, there won't be anywhere to hide," she said.

"Then we've somehow got to find a ride before he turns around again."

Her mind started automatically calculating their odds. A half a mile to the clearing, more or less. Walking four miles an hour meant they'd reach the open in less than ten minutes. They'd seen two cars pass in thirty minutes, and on top of that Nicu was still out there looking for them.

They started walking again, this time staying as far away from the road as possible. She shivered in the cold wind, feeling tired and hungry.

"I can't stop thinking about my father. I can't shake the guilt—"

"Kayla, look at me. None of this is your fault. There was nothing you could have done differently to stop this from happening. You've told me about the security precautions you and your team took."

"It wasn't enough."

"You're not the only one who knows what it's like to feel guilty when everything you plan goes wrong."

She glanced behind them while she waited for him to continue, thankful that for the moment there was still no sign of Nicu.

He nodded. "One of my responsibilities while I was overseas was sending convoys. Our team spent time tracking the enemy's activity and then analyzing which route our men should take."

"And something went wrong?"

"The convoy was hit and we lost two good men."

"What happened? Was your intel wrong?"

"No, but sometimes you do everything you can and things still go wrong." He stopped and brushed a strand of hair away from her cheek. "We're going to do everything we can to find Max, Kayla. I promise."

She nodded, praying he was right. She

heard a car engine and glanced back down the road.

"Levi, there's a car coming, but it's not Nicu."

Different color. Different model.

She waited, her heart pounding, as he stepped out into the road in order to stop the car.

The Mercedes slid to a stop beside him, and an older woman with short gray hair rolled down her window.

Kayla glanced back down the road. The black sedan had turned around and was headed back toward them. They had seconds at the most until Nicu spotted them.

"Levi…"

"Are the two of you okay?" the woman asked, in Dutch.

"Do you speak English?" Levi asked.

"Yes…of course. I was just noticing how you're pretty far out in the country with no transportation."

"Levi, we need to go now."

"We're in a bit of a hurry, but we just need a ride into Amsterdam if you wouldn't mind giving us a lift."

"Well, I happen to be heading in that direction. I'm going as far as Westpoort and can take you there."

"That would be perfect. Thank you."

He held open the door for Kayla before the woman could respond and slid into the car, praying Nicu hadn't seen them.

Kayla's phone buzzed again as the woman started driving. She pulled it out of her pocket and checked her messages.

"Who was it?" Levi asked as he buckled up his seat belt.

"It's Mercy this time." Kayla's eyes were watering when she glanced up at him. "She figured out from my message that something was wrong. She's on her way to the safe house."

Levi's fingers gripped the armrest as he glanced out the back window. They had narrowly managed to escape Nicu and had found Mercy, for which he was grateful, but they definitely weren't out of the woods yet. Not by a long shot. And while he'd prefer not to involve the Good Samaritan who'd just offered them a lift, if Nicu had seen them get into the car, it might make that move unavoidable.

He shifted his attention momentarily to their driver. She was in her sixties and dressed as if she were headed to a party with her white gloves and fashionable hat. What had him worried, though, was the fact that she was driving at least ten miles an hour below the speed limit. He had a feeling she wasn't going to react well to his telling her they needed to hurry because there might be a man involved in a human trafficking ring closing in behind them.

"I know this is going to sound like an odd question," he said, "but would you mind telling us how far we are from the city?"

He saw her brow narrow slightly at the question as she glanced into the rearview mirror.

"Forty minutes or so. Are the two of you okay?"

Levi glanced at Kayla, unsure of how to answer. "We're fine. We just need to get back to Amsterdam."

"So are you the new owners?"

"I'm sorry," Kayla said. "The new owners of what?"

"Of the Brouwer estate, of course. Normally I don't pick up strangers off the road, but when I saw you walking in front of the property, I figured your car must have broken down. And since we're neighbors, I couldn't just drive on by. But I had no idea foreigners had bought the place."

"We were just…guests, actually," Kayla said.

"From where, then? Let me guess—you're Canadians? Americans?"

"Americans," he said, hoping to leave it at that.

"I'm Beverly Meijer," she said.

Levi and Kayla introduced themselves as well, trying to sound more like they were simply on a drive through the countryside and not running from a couple of crazed kidnappers.

"I was born in Texas, actually," the woman rattled on, apparently not noticing the edge to his voice. "Met my husband during a semester abroad. My parents thought I was insane when I told them what I planned to do. We were married four decades until he passed away last year. Lived here my entire adult life. Now I can't imagine not living here."

"This is a beautiful area," Kayla said.

"The Brouwer place used to be one of these beautiful country estates," the woman continued in her singsong voice. "I've dropped by a couple times trying to meet whoever moved in, but no one ever answers the gate. I finally decided the owner is a wealthy hermit, though I suppose I can understand one's need for anonymity. When my husband and I retired, we chose to move away from the city for a bit more peace and quiet. Though I admit there are days I imagine I'd prefer the convenience of the city to the isolation of the country."

"You knew the previous owner?" Kayla asked.

"Of course. The grounds were immaculately kept, and the house itself was like a museum. Cobus Brouwer held the best parties every summer. I never missed them. He'd bring in local musicians and set up a large buffet for his guests. But then his wife died and the parties stopped, and he never seemed to be the same again. He eventually passed away as well, which is what started that ridiculous dispute between his heirs. Not that either of them would have sunk a dime into fixing up the place. Though if you know the new owners of the house, I'm sure you've heard all about the drama and how the house was eventually put up for auction. And by the way, if the new owners happen to be looking for someone to redecorate the place, I have a friend who did my house. She's a bit expensive but has an eye for detail that's unbelievable…"

The woman's voice faded as Levi glanced out the back window. A vehicle was following them, but it wasn't close enough for him to determine the color or make. Coincidence?

He simply wasn't sure. He didn't want to be paranoid, but neither could he be 100 percent certain Nicu hadn't seen them getting into the car.

Kayla gripped his hand. "Do you think he's behind us?" she whispered.

"Honestly, I don't know."

"He has no reason to come after us. Why give us another twenty-four hours just to follow us?"

He wanted to reassure her she was right and that Nicu had no reason to follow them. That Nicu was going to keep his word and let them find Mercy on their own. Except he didn't believe any of that. Already the man had managed to stalk her to ensure she was following their explicit instructions. And he'd bugged her phone. Calling her could have easily been nothing more than his trying to trace her phone and secure their location.

"If they are behind us," he said, "which I'm pretty sure they are, we're going to have to tell her what's going on."

"I know."

He glanced out the window again. If it was Nicu, what was his plan? Biding his time until they stopped? Planning to run them off the road?

"Is everything okay?" The woman's words

broke into his thoughts as they finally approached the city. "The two of you seem... on edge."

Levi glanced at Kayla, whose face had paled. "We've had a rough couple days, but we'd rather not get you involved, ma'am."

"Fiddlesticks. My husband was a *Hoofdcommissaris*—in English you'd call him a chief commissioner. He conducted the day-to-day management of the police force. Anyway, he always used to tell me that he didn't want me involved, which I always thought was ridiculous. The day I married him I was involved."

Kayla squeezed Levi's hand. "We need to tell her. If it is him..."

He knew she was right, but the last thing they needed was more collateral damage.

"We weren't actually guests at the estate like we implied," Levi said finally, then as briefly as possible he explained what had happened over the past twelve hours, including their kidnapping from outside the tram to their eventual escape from the property that had landed them in Beverly's vehicle.

"I knew something fishy was going on at that estate. In fact, I told my best friend Angela just last week, mark my words, we're going to discover one day that something illegal is going on in that house, with all the comings and goings in the night these past few weeks. I can see car headlights as they pull into the drive shining in my bedroom window. And those dogs…they never stop barking when people show up."

Kayla leaned forward and rested her arm on the top of the seat in front of her. "Did you ever see who was coming and going?"

"They mostly came at night, so no. But every couple weeks the dogs start barking and I know they're back. But human trafficking? I never imagined something like that. No wonder you're in a hurry to get to the city." She started digging in her purse. "My cell phone's in here somewhere. You can call the police."

"I'm not sure we should do that," Levi said.

"Why not?"

"For the same reason we can't let you get involved. There's just too much at stake for us not to do what they are demanding. And they told us not to get the authorities involved."

"But I have connections. People I know that can be trusted."

Levi caught the spark of hope registering in Kayla's eyes. At some point they were going to need to get outside help, but right now he didn't believe it was worth the risk of getting her father killed.

"Surely I can do something," Beverly said. "If you're not going to the police, then where are you going?"

"If you can drop us near the city center, we'll be able to figure out a way out of this."

Levi glanced behind them as Beverly drove into the outskirts of the city. The car that had been behind them had slowly bridged the gap, and now there was no longer any doubt that the vehicle following them was Nicu's.

"After I lose the sedan behind us?" Beverly asked as they approached the city.

Levi hesitated. "I'm sorry to have dragged you into this, but yes. That would help."

"Then hang on."

Levi grabbed the armrest as Beverly pushed on the accelerator. The sedan behind them sped up as well, staying barely a car length behind them.

Beverly turned onto a narrow street that ran along one of the canals, trying to avoid pedestrians and bicyclists in the process.

A moment later, the other vehicle smashed into the back of the Mercedes. Their car skidded forward while Beverly fought to keep the car on the road.

"Beverly?"

"I'm okay," she said, still gripping the steering wheel, "but what in the world is he trying to do?"

Levi felt any ounce of remaining control vanish as he braced for a second impact. "He's trying to push us into the canal."

TWELVE

Levi felt the impact of the other vehicle as it slammed into the back of the Mercedes a second time, shoving their car precariously close to the edge of the canal. Beverly pressed on the accelerator while swerving to the left and somehow managed to prevent the anticipated nosedive into the water. But a glance behind them confirmed that Nicu had no intention of backing down.

"Try getting us away from the canal," he said, wishing he could somehow take control of the situation and put an end to it.

Beverly sped forward, then at the last minute took a sharp left up another narrow street. Behind them the sedan, following too closely, missed the turn and instead slammed into another vehicle parked along the edge of the canal. Levi watched as the compact car teetered for a couple seconds on the edge of the street above the canal, then plunged into the water below.

Beverly took advantage of the situation and put distance between them, while Nicu struggled to back up and catch up with them. But two blocks later the Mercedes lost power and died.

"Beverly…" Kayla grabbed Levi's arm, her fingernails digging into his skin.

"I don't know what's wrong." She tried to restart the car. "The engine won't turn over."

He caught the look of panic in Kayla's eyes.

The accident had already caught the attention of a number of people who'd been walking along the canal, and within a matter of minutes, a crowd had gathered near the road and around the side of the sedan, blocking their way. Jumping out of the passenger side, Nicu and his partner abandoned their vehicle and started sprinting away from the canal.

"You both need to get out of here now," Beverly said. "There are enough people around, and I'm sure the police are already on their way."

"We can't just leave you here," Kayla said.

"And besides that, your car—" Levi started.

"Don't worry about me or my car," Beverly said. "Now go."

Staying would be dangerous, so Levi

thanked the woman then slipped out of the car ahead of Kayla. Together they hurried in the opposite direction from the crowd that now had their attention focused on the car that was floating in the canal.

"Did you see which way Nicu went?" she asked.

"I think they headed west, but we have no way to know where they are now."

She was still holding on to his arm as they hurried down the cobbled sidewalks lined with tiny boutiques selling vintage clothes and embroidered Dutch farmhouse table-cloths and linens. They passed rows of skinny houses and a sprinkling of cafés, with outdoor seating catering to customers willing to brave the low temperatures. Reggae played from a coffee shop across the street. Levi breathed in the scent of freshly baked bread, remind-ing him that neither of them had eaten since the night before. But he couldn't even think about eating right now.

"We're not far from the safe house," she said, "but I don't think it's wise to go straight there. Not if there's a chance they could spot us."

"Agreed."

Which meant if Nicu *was* anywhere nearby, they needed to find him first.

Sirens buzzed in the background. Someone must have called the authorities about the accident, which helped ease the guilt of leaving their Good Samaritan behind. But he doubted Nicu was interested in talking to Beverly. At this point, his only objective was going to be to find them and, in turn, Mercy.

So much for Nicu giving them twenty-four hours to find Mercy. Apparently he'd never intended to just let them go.

"I don't see them," Kayla said, gripping Levi's forearm even tighter.

"I don't, either." He glanced behind him, looking for Nicu's tall, lean frame. "But there are so many people. For now, let's just concentrate on putting as much distance between them and us as we can."

He wrapped his arm around her waist, wanting this nightmare to be over. Because he couldn't help but wonder what it would be like to explore the city with her without anyone after them. Wondered what it would be like to sit down at one of the cafés and have dinner together, or to take one of the canal cruises at night. Because part of him still wanted to get to know Kayla again, and to find out more about the woman she'd become.

But that wasn't why he was here. He was

here to keep her safe, and that's exactly what he intended to do.

"Who runs the safe house," he asked, keeping his arm around her as they maneuvered down the busy sidewalk.

"It's above a café that's been in a local family for five generations. Their daughter was murdered two decades ago, so they're emotionally invested in our program. It's how they originally got involved in what we're doing. The girls are taught to memorize the number to the safe house and to always keep a phone card with them. If for some reason they can't get to the safe house, they can call from a public phone anywhere in the city, and someone from our team will pick them up."

"That's a lot of security precautions you have in place," he said, glancing behind him. There was still no sign of Nicu or his brother.

"We tried to think of everything." Kayla slowed down in front of a bakery. "The safe house is only a block away. But if we're being followed…"

He scanned the dozens of pedestrians bustling down the street. A woman pushing a baby carriage, along with couples, shoppers and businesspeople, while those on bikes sped past them in the red cycling lane.

But there was still no sign of Nicu.

A tram bell rang from the adjacent street as it passed them. From what Kayla had told him, the safe house had been chosen primarily for its easy connection to city transport. And for the couple who'd agreed to take in the girls if ever they were in trouble.

"Let's go ahead and go there. The longer we're on the street, the more of a chance there is they'll spot us."

A minute later, they stepped inside one of the dozens of cafés sprinkled across the city, where regulars were currently catching up on a football match in front of old-fashioned open hearth. Stone floor, beamed ceilings, a cozy wood interior and wooden barrels over the bar completed the old European look.

Kayla hurried through the café without stopping, leading them to the back of the building and an inconspicuous flight of stairs. At the top, she knocked on the door with a peephole that was opened then promptly locked behind them.

Kayla hesitated briefly inside the small entryway before embracing her friend. "Celine, it's so good to see you."

"And you as well, though never for this reason."

Kayla quickly introduced Levi to Celine. "Has she said anything to you?"

"Not really." Their host nodded toward the couch on the other side of the room at a young girl who didn't look a day over fourteen. "I gave her some tea, hoping she would sleep for a while, but for the most part, she's just been staring out the window."

Mercy sat cross-legged on a couch, her hair neatly braided in thin rows down her back. A strong wave of compassion washed over him, because Mercy's sense of safety and security were gone. And for her it wasn't the first time.

Kayla felt her eyes well with tears as she pulled Mercy into her arms. She might not have any idea at this point how they were going to save both Mercy and her father, but for right now the only thing that mattered was that the girl was safe.

"I'm so sorry," Mercy said, looking up at her with her wide, almond-shaped dark eyes.

"Stop." Kayla pulled her back into her arms and hugged her tightly, her own eyes filling with tears. "You have nothing to be sorry for. I'm just glad you're safe. I've been so worried."

"I know I should have come here first, but I was afraid he was following me. Afraid of what he would do if he caught me, so I just kept running."

"You're safe now. He can't find you here."

"Maybe not, but he's smart. If he wants to find me, he will. But I know I never should have left, because leaving only put you and the other girls at risk."

"Mercy, this isn't your fault. None of it. You need to know that."

Kayla turned around to where Levi stood, her arm still tight around Mercy's shoulders. "I want you to meet Levi. He's a friend of mine. We grew up together, actually, and he's here to help."

"It's nice to meet you, Mercy," Levi said, shaking her hand.

She shot him a timid smile. "It's nice to meet you as well."

Kayla motioned the two of them to the couch. "While I wish this was a happy reunion, there are some questions we need to ask you."

Kayla caught the fear in her eyes as Mercy drew in a deep breath and nodded. "Okay."

Kayla sat down on the couch next to Mercy while Levi took the empty chair across from them. "We know Nicu is trying to get you back. Can you tell me when you last saw him?"

Mercy's gaze dropped. "Yesterday morning. I was riding the tram to work, and he was there. At the back of the tram. I thought I had just imagined him following me. Thought I was paranoid. I don't know how he found me."

"What happened next?"

She shook her head. "I jumped off the tram, but he followed me and grabbed my arm. Told me he had been looking for me. He insisted that I come with him because I still belonged to him."

"But you got away?"

Mercy's lip quivered. "I… I started screaming and ran. And somehow I lost him in the crowd."

It was what they'd told the girls to do if they ever felt their life was in danger. But it was also something that would have made Nicu angry.

Kayla squeezed her hand, knowing that the day was replaying in Mercy's mind. That day and probably a dozen others.

"You should have called me."

"I know, but I didn't want you to get involved. He would kill you if he knew you were trying to keep me from him." Mercy drew in a ragged breath. "He's done it before."

Everything was starting to come together. This *was* more than just a matter of money for Nicu. He was obsessed.

Celine quietly set a plate of *kroketten*—deep-fried rolls with meat ragout inside—and a second plate of *stroopwafels*, Dutch cookies made from thin layers of waffles filled with a sticky syrup, and a pot of hot chocolate on the table.

Kayla smiled up at her friend. "Thank you."

"Please continue talking, but I have the feeling that all three of you need to eat something. I've also updated your team on what's going on, so you don't have to worry about that. They've been worried about you. I'll be back in a second with plates and cups."

Kayla thanked her while Mercy stared at the food.

"I'm not sure if I can."

"When's the last time you ate?" Kayla asked.

"I don't remember."

"Then just try," Kayla said.

Mercy picked up one of the waffles but only nibbled on the edge before setting it down on one of the plates Celine brought.

"You said you believed that someone had been following you?" Kayla asked, pressing for more information. "I'm assuming it was Nicu."

Mercy nodded. "There were a couple of

strange calls and a few text messages. I knew it was him. I tried to convince myself he couldn't find me, that he was still in Italy. But I was wrong."

"Do you still have your phone?" Kayla asked.

"Yes…it's…it's in my backpack."

"If you'll let Levi look at it, he'll make sure you can't be traced."

Mercy grabbed her backpack off the floor, pulled out her phone, then hesitated.

"It's okay, Mercy. You can trust him."

Levi took the phone, then stood up. "Thanks, Mercy. I'll go work on it over by the window where there's better light."

Kayla nodded at his understanding. Trust didn't come easily for girls like Mercy.

"What happens now?" Mercy asked.

"We'll work on a plan, but you'll be safe here for now. And in the meantime, you could take a nap in the guest room, if you'd like. I'm sure you're exhausted."

Mercy fiddled with one of the straps of her backpack. "There's something you're not telling me."

"What do you mean?"

"Has something happened to one of the other girls?"

"The girls are fine."

"Then what is it? Because I know Nicu. I've seen what he will do when he wants something."

Kayla hesitated, not wanting to pile guilt on top of everything Mercy was already trying to deal with. But it was something she would find out eventually.

"They took my father," Kayla said. "They thought they could use him for leverage to get me to find you. But I don't want you to worry. We found you, and we'll find a way to get him back as well."

Mercy's fingers dug into the backpack in her lap. "So Nicu wants to trade me for your father."

"We would never do that, Mercy."

"Then how will you get him back? Nicu won't just hand him over to be nice."

"I'm not sure yet what we're going to do, but we'll figure it out."

"No..." Mercy dropped the strap of the backpack, then stood up. "No. This needs to end. I won't sacrifice anyone's life for mine. I'm going to go back to Nicu."

Kayla stood up and stepped in front of Mercy. "Forget it. There's no way we will let you do that. We will find a way to keep both of you safe."

She shook her head. "You don't understand. This *is* the only way. He won't just let this go."

"Listen to me, Mercy." Kayla rested her hands on the girl's shoulders and looked her in the eyes. "When you came into our program, we agreed to do everything we could to keep you safe. Nothing has changed. We're going to figure out a way to keep both of you safe."

Mercy pulled away, then tugged on her shirt so her shoulder was exposed. There was a bar code tattooed across her dark skin, like an item label in a grocery store. Below them were the initials *ND*. "You know what this is."

Kayla stared at the markings, her heart breaking.

"It's a brand," Mercy continued. "A brand that tells everyone that I'm his property. Nicu Dragan. A war wound that will never let me forget what happened to me. You convinced me that I could simply walk away from him. Told me I could be free, but now…look what my walking away has done. And now if your father or one of you die because of me…"

Kayla bit the edge of her lip, at a loss for what to say. Branding the girls was a way of taking away their humanity. Something that had been done to people throughout history, from Roman slaves to Auschwitz prisoners to today's sex-trafficking victims.

Mercy had become his property, and even though she'd found a way to run, nothing had changed for Nicu. Branding had become a way to control the girls, to compel them to do what he wanted. Gangs, violence, rapes... And because the crime was so lucrative, it had become a never-ending epidemic. Some people, like Lilly, would never find freedom. But there was still hope for Mercy, and there was nothing she could do or say that would convince Kayla to send her back to Nicu.

"You cannot tell me this isn't my fault. Your father was abducted because of me." Mercy grabbed Kayla's hands, exposing the rope burns where Nicu had tied her up. "And this... What did he do to you?"

"It doesn't matter."

"Doesn't it?" Mercy rubbed her forehead with the palm of her hand, the anxiety clear in her eyes, then sat back down on the couch. "I always knew he would kill me. Every day I waited for the moment when he'd beat me to the point where I didn't wake up. And when it didn't happen, I thought about killing myself."

"But you didn't."

"No. The hope of one day getting back

to my family kept me going. Knowing how much my mother would hurt if I didn't try to fight to stay alive. But now…now it would be better off if I were dead. Then none of this would have ever happened. I wouldn't have hurt any of you."

"Mercy, no." Kayla caught the sadness in her eyes. "Everything you're listening to in your head right now is a lie."

"Is it? I don't think God can forgive me for what I've done." She glanced at a blue delft vase on a shelf on the other side of the living room. "I'm like a piece of shattered pottery, and I don't think it's possible to put me back together again."

THIRTEEN

Kayla walked out of the guest room where Mercy had finally agreed to try to get some rest and quietly shut the door behind her. Levi sat at the table working through the files he'd taken from Nicu's office, while she could see Celine scrubbing down the counters in the adjacent kitchen.

"Is Mercy okay?" Levi asked, standing up.

"She's sleeping now. She's exhausted."

"So are you." He reached out and squeezed her shoulder gently.

"I'll be fine. We don't exactly have time to rest." She glanced at the clock hanging on the wall. "We have until tomorrow to come up with an answer to save them both. And besides, you're the one suffering from jet lag."

He didn't look convinced by her argument. "Why don't you at least lie down for an hour?"

"I'm not sure I could sleep...even if I

wanted to." She picked up Mercy's cell phone off the table. "What did you find?"

"I've taken it off, but I did find spyware on it."

"How? She said he found her, but she got away. Far as I know, he couldn't have had access to her cell."

"He wouldn't have to."

She dropped the phone back on the table. "What do you mean?"

"All it takes is someone to connect remotely to your phone via the internet with a cell phone spy app."

His answer sent a chill through her. How were they supposed to get out of this? "I'm scared, Levi."

He motioned her to sit down next to him. "Tell me what you're thinking."

"We work with these girls for months. Counseling them, giving them spiritual direction…everything we can to ensure that not only are they safe, but that they begin to heal emotionally." She pulled her legs up underneath her. "But sometimes…sometimes we can't stop what's happening to them. And sometimes the wounds run too deep."

Like pieces of shattered pottery.

Kayla let out a soft *whoosh* of air. Mercy's words had dug deep into her own fractured heart. Meeting the girls' physical needs wasn't the only thing that had to be dealt with. But sometimes, everything they did to help put the girls back together again wasn't enough.

He glanced at her, catching her gaze. "I'm going to keep looking in these files for something we can use for leverage."

"But what if that isn't enough? What if I can't save my father? What if it's already too late?"

Levi hesitated before answering. "God gave man free will, and unfortunately that means we sometimes suffer from the consequences of other people's actions. But God uses people like you, who can fight for truth and justice. People who are willing to stand for God's grace and freedom and risk everything. As I recall, there were a few people in the Bible who thought the same thing. Moses... Gideon... Esther... It seems like God's pretty good at using ordinary—and even sometimes inadequate—people."

Like Corrie ten Boom.

How had she let herself forget?

"You reminded me of someone," she said, speaking her thoughts out loud. "You've heard of Corrie ten Boom, the woman whose family hid Jews during World War II?"

"Yes."

"She lived with her father and sister above their watch shop in Haarlem, not far from here, for fifty years. She was a licensed watchmaker."

An ordinary woman who made watches.

"Her story's one of the reasons I'm here right now," she continued. "My mother read her story to me when I was in junior high. Later, while we were still searching for Lilly, I started volunteering with a friend. After we found Lilly's body, I kept volunteering and eventually did an internship, working with teenage trafficking victims. Fast-forward a few years, when the organization decided to branch into Europe, and they asked me to work here. I always found it ironic, a sort of coming full circle, because I never forgot Corrie ten Boom's story and how God used her. I guess I hoped that God would use me. I just never expected my own life to be in danger."

And in the process she'd let fear completely take over.

"God's involvement in something doesn't mean it's risk-free," he said. "In fact, most of the time it's the opposite."

Kayla glanced back at the blue-and-white vase on the shelf. "My mother visited me here before she died. One afternoon we visited Corrie ten Boom's home. I never forgot that visit. When I look at the girls, I can't help thinking about them and the fear they live with every day."

"But God is using you, and you are making a difference. And that's what you can't forget."

Maybe.

"Thank you for being here. Because if you hadn't come…"

She glanced up at him and took in his familiar eyes and the curve of his jawline. Levi was a friend and would never be more than that. But if that was true, then why was her heart racing at his nearness?

She turned away, needing to distance herself from him and the feelings he invoked. "Would you like some tea? I could really use some tea right now."

"Sure, but first…would you mind if I used your phone? I'd like to watch the video of your father again."

Kayla pulled the phone from her pocket and handed it to him before escaping into the kitchen where Celine was now busy scrubbing the stove.

"You've just discovered one of my secrets," Celine said, wringing out her sponge in the sink. "I clean when I'm upset. Jansen always knows he better watch out if he comes home to a sparkling house."

Kayla laughed and felt some of the tension break. "I clean out my closets and cupboards when I'm upset. And drink tea. You don't mind if I make some tea, do you?"

"Of course not," Celine said. "If you'll get the water going, I'll get the tea and sugar out."

Kayla poured water into the electric kettle then flipped it on. "Thank you, Celine. For everything."

"Of course. Jansen and I hoped this day would never come, but if it did, we were determined to be ready."

"We couldn't do what we do without people like you who are willing to risk so much for these girls."

Celine shook her head. "I can't imagine not helping. I grew up hearing stories of the underground network from my mother. My grandmother was an *onderduiker*—in English it literally means under-diver, or a person in hiding. Those who were involved in hiding refugees and enemies of Hitler's regime."

A sliver of anger shot through Kayla. She'd read stories from the Dutch Resistance of hundreds of Jewish children smuggled from a preschool and others who were hidden at the zoo, in the backs of warehouses, behind secret passages. The men and women who, like Celine's grandmother, had lost their lives as part of the Resistance to save the lives of the Jews. Those who had to hide from men wanting to take their lives just because of who they were. Had anything truly changed?

"Why haven't we learned enough to stop this from happening?" Kayla asked. "Things like this aren't supposed to happen today. People are supposed to look at history and learn from the horrors others lived through."

"I've asked myself that question more than once." Celine pulled down a box of tea from the cupboard, then reached for the sugar. "During the time of the Resistance, the Nazis hunted Jewish families in order to throw them into concentration camps. More than three hundred thousand were taken into hiding— tens of thousands of landlords and caretakers helped hide the people. Identity papers were forged, along with intelligence work to ensure the safety of those in hiding."

And here they were again, over half a century later, facing the same situation. It was like it was happening all over again.

"Do you think she'll be okay?" Celine asked.

"I don't know. I think the only way to end

it—at least for Mercy—is ensure Nicu and everyone he works with are in custody."

"Which will happen. It has to." Celine touched her arm as the water in the electric kettle started heating. "Can I ask you a personal question?"

"Of course."

"This is off topic, but I was wondering about Levi. I enjoyed talking with him for a few minutes while you were in with Mercy."

Kayla glanced back into the adjoining living room, where Levi continued going through the files they'd brought with them. She wondered exactly what they'd talked about. "He's just an old friend from back home. We grew up together, though he's a bit older than me."

"Only a friend?" Celine asked.

"Yes. Why?"

"I don't know. There's something about the way he talks about you. I thought there might have once been something between you."

"No. And besides, I… I haven't seen him for years."

"Is that why you blush when he looks at you or when I mention his name?"

"You're imagining things."

"Am I?"

She didn't want to think about their past.

"Seeing him again just brings up lots of memories. But none of that really matters. He'll leave soon, and I probably won't see him again."

But was that what she really wanted?

She set a teabag in the empty cup. Of course it was.

"All I want to do right now is ensure Mercy and my father are safe."

"And all I am saying," Celine said, "is that when you find that one person, don't let him go. Trust me. It's worth it."

"Kayla?" Levi stepped into the kitchen, his hands shoved into his back pockets. "I'm sorry to interrupt, but I think I've found something."

Levi caught the worry lines etched across Kayla's forehead. The kettle bubbled in the background as she braced her hands against the counter like she was waiting for another bombshell to drop. She might not think she was courageous, but he knew the truth. Not only did he now know what she did on a day-to-day basis, he'd seen her deal with Ana and Mercy. There was a compassion in her voice when she spoke to them, and a willingness to risk her own life to ensure their safety. As far as he was concerned, God had brought her to this place for such a time as this.

"What's going on?" she asked.

"Go on and talk to him," Celine urged. "I'll finish up with the tea, then bring it out in a couple minutes."

Kayla nodded her thanks, then followed Levi back into the living room, where she sat down on the edge of the couch.

He glanced at the stack of files spread out across the table before answering her question, trying to decide on the best way to tell her what he'd come up with. In the army, his job had been to take the information given them and come up with a strategy regarding the enemy, including their size, position and the likely course of action they would take. They had to determine not only what the enemy *could* do, but what they *would* do. And how circumstances affected that information.

In reality, this was the same situation. They needed to determine not only what Nicu could do, but what he would do. And how far he was willing to go to get Mercy back. But Kayla wasn't going to like what he'd come up with.

"Levi, what's going on?"

He sat down next to her. "I've been going through the files, looking for something that would force Nicu to walk away without us having to go to the police and risk Max's life."

"And you found something?"

"Not exactly. But I listened to your conversation with Mercy," he said, leaning forward. "And the bottom line is I don't think it matters what we have on Nicu, because I don't think he will ever just walk away. This isn't about making a profit. He wants Mercy back. He sees her as his property, yes, but there's also something far more than that. Anyone who gets in the way is completely inconsequential to him. And because he's not thinking like a businessman, he's not willing to cut his losses when things go bad."

"So leverage won't work," Kayla said.

"I don't think so. We have to take their leverage out of the equation."

"Okay, but how are we supposed to do that?"

Levi hesitated before answering her question. "I think I might know where your father is."

Kayla stopped pacing and caught his gaze. "Are you serious?"

"I need you to listen to the video Nicu sent you again."

"Levi, I can't—"

"I'm sorry. I know this isn't easy, but there's a reason for I'm asking you to do this."

Kayla sat back down next to him, clearly disturbed by his request. "What am I listening for?"

"The bells in the background." He grabbed her phone off the table. "I need to know if you recognize them."

He found the video, then pushed Play, wishing he didn't have to ask her to watch this again.

I'm so sorry...demanding that you hand over one of your girls...twenty-four hours... they will kill me.

"Well?" He switched off the phone. "Do you want me to play it again? Or maybe we could ask Celine—"

"No. I recognize the bells, and I don't know how I missed that before. They're from the Westerkerk on the bank of the Prinsengracht. The big church on the canal near the Anne Frank House."

"You're sure?"

"Definitely."

"So there would be houseboats nearby?" he asked.

"Lots of them."

"Okay, now this is just an educated guess,

but I think I can to track your father to a house-boat along one of the canals near the church."

"Wait a minute…you really think he might be on a houseboat?"

"I found a rental agreement in the files for a houseboat that's just a couple blocks from the Westerkerk, so it fits. I might be off, but it's the closest thing we have to a lead at the moment."

He wanted to assure her that if they showed up at the houseboat, her father would be there and he'd be okay. But he knew there could be no guarantees.

"What I'm worried about is how easy it would be to move the boat to a new location," Levi said. "All they'd have to do is keep moving the boat, and we'd never find him."

Kayla shook her head. "They can move him, but not the boat. I had a friend who owned a houseboat. Most of the money you spend is for the mooring. Meaning you can't just buy a boat and park it wherever you want. It's a well-documented and organized system. And while they might be able to move my father to a new location, moving the boat itself would be much more complicated."

"Okay, so if I'm right about the mooring location, then there's a good chance that we'll be able to find your father. But we need to get the police involved."

"I agree."

"You do?"

"Yes," she said, "but I think that means we need further proof he's there before we call them. It also means that we're going to have to work fast. If it gets back to Nicu that the police are involved and we don't know where he is, they will kill my father."

Which meant they had to find him quickly.

Celine opened the front door, letting in a man Levi recognized from a photo in the living room.

Levi caught the panic in Celine's eyes. "This is my husband, Jansen."

"We've got a problem," he said, rushing into the room. "There are two men downstairs. I don't know how they found us, but one of them matches the description you gave Celine of the man after Mercy. One of my employees is trying to stall them, but they're carrying weapons."

Levi's mind raced through possible scenarios. "If we're not careful, this could quickly escalate into a hostage situation."

"Agreed," Jansen said.

Celine grabbed her phone. "The police need to be involved."

"I've just called them," her husband said, "and they're on their way."

"But Nicu could find us before they get here," Kayla said.

"Do you have an emergency exit strategy?" Levi asked.

"Yes," Celine said. "There's a back way out of here."

"Then, Kayla, go get Mercy. We need to get out of here now."

FOURTEEN

It only took a fraction of a second for the gravity of the situation to sink in and leave Kayla feeling as if she couldn't breathe. But the swift panic that followed was automatically sidetracked as Kayla's brain switched into survival gear. She knew exactly what to do. This was what they'd planned for.

"How did they find us?" Celine asked her husband.

"I don't know."

The reality was, it didn't matter how they'd found them. The clock was ticking before Nicu and his men decided to check the upstairs apartment.

"Celine, get the emergency backpack," Kayla said. "I'll wake up Mercy. We need to get out of here now."

"Our car's in the shop," Jansen said as she crossed the living room. "Which is going to make this more complicated."

Kayla frowned, but there was no time to worry about what they couldn't change. "Then we'll go with plan B and take the ferry to the other safe house."

It had to work. It was the only option they had at the moment.

"I'll get the tickets." Jansen headed for a desk in the corner of the room, making Kayla extra grateful that they'd gone through every scenario they could think of in advance.

She stepped into room where Mercy was softly snoring. She'd been through so much already, but clearly this was far from over.

We need to find a way to end this, God. Permanently.

"Mercy." Kayla shook her gently. "I'm sorry, but we need to leave quickly. Here's your coat and scarf. Your boots are on the floor next to the bed."

Mercy let out a soft groan, then sat up. "What happened?"

"Nicu's downstairs. We need to hurry and get out of here."

She grabbed one of her boots. "How did he find me?"

Kayla scooped up the second boot and set it next to her. "It doesn't matter at this point. We just need to get out of here."

Mercy tugged on her boots. "I knew I shouldn't have turned on my phone. That has to be how he found me."

"None of that matters now. Only getting out of here safely. And that's exactly what we're going to do, Mercy. We're going to get you somewhere he can't find you."

Mercy didn't hesitate as she finished putting on her other boot, then stood up and slipped on her coat. They'd planned out every detail and practiced their escape in case there was ever a danger of their being discovered here at the safe house. They knew exactly what to do. Two minutes was the maximum time they'd have to get out of here before someone downstairs found them.

They headed toward the living room, where Celine was pulling out prepared go bags filled with cash, burner phones, nonperishables like *pindakaas*—Dutch peanut butter—crackers and granola bars. There were changes of clothes and extra jackets and scarves. Kayla had always prayed they'd never have to use the stash. Because now they were going to have to test the two-minute theory in a real-world emergency. And they were already down to half that.

Please, God. Let it be enough.

"I've got the go bags and tickets," Levi said. He was used to doing the planning for missions. This time he was clearly trying to keep up with what was going on. "What's the actual plan out of here?"

"We've got less than sixty seconds." She glanced at the clock in the corner of the room and grabbed her coat and scarf. "The ferry station's right around the corner. There's a secret exit out of the building through the attics that run atop the other apartments and eventually leads to another street. If we can get there without them finding us, we should be all right."

"What else can I do?" Levi asked.

"We'll catch the ferry and take Mercy to the second safe house we have set up," Kayla said. "Then we'll see about finding my father."

"I've already sent Rene the signal," Jansen said. "He knows you're coming and will be ready."

"Wait a minute." Celine hesitated while her husband opened the secret door to the attic that was hidden behind the coats in the front closet. "More than likely, they'll be looking for the three of you. Let me take Mercy to the safe house. Jansen will stay here and wait for the police. And, Kayla… I heard you and

Levi talking. The two of you need to go find your father."

"Forget it, Celine," Kayla said. "It's too dangerous."

Celine took a step forward. "I don't care. We didn't sign up for this because I thought it was a walk in the park. We agreed to let you use our home because we believe in what you're doing. Because we want to make sure these girls stay safe."

"Celine—"

"I can get her safely to Rene's without a tail. I've been through all the training the girls have had, and it will give you a head start in finding your father."

Kayla glanced at Levi, who nodded at her. She wanted to agree, but would she be sacrificing both Mercy and Celine for the sake of her father?

"Please, Kayla."

There was no time to argue. "Promise you'll call us as soon as you're safe."

"I will."

Kayla glanced at the plates of food still sitting on the table, then turned to Jansen. "Make sure there is no sign that the three of us were here, in case they force their way inside. And you're going to need to stall them until the police arrive. Redirect them. Anything you can think of to ensure they don't follow us."

"I can do that. Go. And be careful. All of you."

Someone banged on the apartment door. Jansen quickly shut the closet door behind them, leaving them in darkness except for thin cracks of light above them. Celine flipped on a flashlight that lit up the narrow staircase into the dark attic with its steep gables that were filled with cobwebs and years of collected dust.

The muscles in Kayla's jaw tensed as they followed Celine, praying that music from the café below was enough to cover up their footsteps. She walked into a spiderweb, then quickly wiped the sticky threads from her face. Even with a flashlight the room felt dark and eerie.

Church bells rang out in the distance, barely audible above the music playing below them.

She shuddered and knew for certain that Nicu and his brother would kill them if they found them.

The chilly crawl space was just tall enough for Levi to walk hunched over like an old man. The yellow beam of the flashlight caught a pile of boxes and a few pieces of forgotten furniture. His muscles tensed. If Nicu discovered where they'd gone and followed them, there would be no place for them to run.

Because one thing was clear from everything that had happened. Nicu would do anything in his power to get Mercy back. Which was why when he'd hesitantly agreed with Celine's argument that she take Mercy to the second safe house, he still had his doubts they'd made the right decision. If Nicu could discover this safe house, who was to say he couldn't find them now?

"There's a staircase that leads down to the ground floor just ahead of us," Celine said. "It ends up along a street on the back side of the block."

Thirty seconds later they were making their way down the narrow staircase that was encased in decades-old brick walls.

"Wait a minute," Levi said as Celine opened the door. "Let's make sure no one's watching this exit."

He slipped outside and immediately wished the guard had been wearing a warmer jacket. While the sun had decided to come out for a bit, a cold wind still whipped around him. But the temperature was the last thing he was worried about at the moment. He needed to ensure they weren't walking into a trap. While there were a few pedestrians enjoying the cold winter afternoon, the cobblestone street appeared quiet. The long row of apartments was lined with bikes locked up by their owners. A Vespa sped past them, but its driver didn't seem to notice them. No one seemed to notice them.

"Which way?" Levi asked.

"At the next intersection, Mercy and I will need to head west," Celine said as they started walking. "The ferry's not far from here. You'll be going in the opposite direction."

"You need to hurry." Kayla squeezed Mercy's hand. "But please…let us know as soon as you are safe. And if something—anything—goes wrong, call the police."

Celine and Mercy hurried toward the ferry, while Levi continued to take in their surroundings. "I don't see Nicu or anyone who looks out of place."

"I don't, either," Kayla said as they started in the opposite direction. "There's a tram that stops right next to the Westerkerk, which will be the quickest way there. We just need to walk a few blocks to catch it."

"How are you doing?" he asked, worried about her as much as he was for Mercy.

"Scared. Nervous. What happens if my father isn't there? What happens if we can't find him?"

It wasn't a question he was ready to answer. His theory on where Nicu was holding her father was an educated guess at best. And even if he'd been in that boat when they'd made the recording, Nicu and his men still could have moved him since then. There was simply no way to know at this point. But second-guessing their only lead wasn't going to help, either.

They kept walking in silence down the busier cross street, past an antique shop selling vintage handbags, a pastry shop and a café.

Kayla stopped in the middle of the sidewalk as a bicycle whizzed past them ringing its bell. "Levi."

"What is it?"

"Thirty yards or so ahead of us is a man wearing a long black coat and a dark blue scarf. He's walking toward us. He was the other man with Nicu at the house. His brother, Andrei."

"I see him." His mind automatically ran through their options as he grabbed her hand

and turned back in the direction they'd come from. "Do you think he saw us?"

She shook her head. "I'm not sure, but we're going to need to find another way to the tram."

Without leading Andrei toward Mercy and Celine.

The worry in his gut continued to gnaw at him. Nicu and Andrei knew they were out here somewhere, and both were intent on finding them. Something Levi couldn't let happen.

"Do we have any idea how many men are actually working with Nicu?" he asked as they sidestepped a woman pushing a baby carriage.

"I only saw Andrei and the guard we confronted, plus whoever broke into the girls' apartment, but the work they do is competitive, so they keep their crews small."

But while he hoped there were only the three of them, there was no way to know how many were looking for them. He glanced behind him and caught sight of the man's blue scarf. They were definitely still being followed.

"And, Levi... Nicu's ahead of us."

This time there was no time to consider a strategy. He led her down the first side street to the right, and together they started running down the narrowing alley. Ahead of them a large truck backed into the other end of the skinny passage, blocking the exit. Levi glanced back, certain that at least one if not both of the men had seen them. Which meant turning around wasn't an option. And now neither was going forward.

They were trapped.

How had he let this happen?

They passed a number of doors as they ran, presumably leading to storefronts. He tried the first door they came to. It was locked. Another ten yards was another door. This one was unlocked.

Levi slipped into the large warehouse-type building with Kayla, locking the door behind them. With no heat inside, the place felt like a freezer. Stepping through a door of plastic sheeting, they found a larger storeroom with fifteen-foot ceilings. From the looks of it, someone had completely gutted the building and was currently in the process of refurbishing it. The room was filled with dozens of cardboard boxes, tall metal scaffolding, paint buckets and more large plastic sheets that had been laid out across the floor.

On the other side of the room, two or three dozen mannequins stood closely together, waiting to be put on display once the store was complete. For now, though, most of them were missing arms and heads, making the dimly lit store feel more like they'd walked into the middle of some science experiment.

"There are no windows in here," Kayla said. "How do we get out?"

"It looks like this room's for storage," Levi said, walking across the plastic sheeting. "But there's got to be access to the front."

Kayla's phone rang in her pocket. She pulled it out and quickly answered it.

"That was Celine," she said quietly as soon as she hung up the call. "She said they made it to the ferry, and there were no signs of anyone following them."

The sound of splitting wood echoed inside the warehouse, interrupting his response. Levi grabbed Kayla's hand and started to run, but it was too late. A bullet pinged off the wall above them as someone shouted for them to stop.

Levi stopped next to the row of mannequins and slowly turned around. Nicu stood in a stream of light from the open door.

FIFTEEN

"Where is she?" Nicu's deep voice bounced off the tall ceilings of the warehouse as he leveled his gun at them.

Kayla tried to capture the tendrils of fear wrapping themselves around her heart as Nicu's brother stepped into the room behind him. The only thing good about this situation was that if both of them were here, they weren't running after Mercy and Celine. But now that they'd found them, she knew they had no intentions of letting them go again.

"We still have another eighteen hours to find her," Levi said, raising his hands beside him.

"I think you already found Mercy," Nicu said. "I found your safe house, and now you're only a couple blocks away? Sounds too convenient if you ask me."

"Was she at the safe house?" Levi asked.

"No, but I think you already know that.

The thing is, you can't hide her and expect me to in turn give up your father, Kayla. That's not how things are going to work."

What do we do, God? Mercy's life for my father's? My father's life for hers? You know I can't do this!

She remembered what Levi had told her. Play the game. Make him believe he was winning.

"Do you actually think I'd put the life of one of your girls above my father's?" she asked. "But Levi's right. You gave us another twenty-four hours to find her. That was the deal."

"Things have changed. I'm tired of your stalling and excuses," Nicu said. "And you know too much. Which is why if you'd never gotten involved in this in the first place none of this would have happened."

"And Mercy? What would have happened to her?" Levi asked.

"She's mine and she always will be."

"She's not a piece of property you can just buy or sell or barter," Kayla said. She was going to forget trying to make him think he'd won. He already believed he'd won no matter what she said.

"You're wrong," he said. "She is mine."

Kayla glanced at Levi. Talking to Nicu wasn't going to get them anywhere.

A loud voice echoed in another part of the building, momentarily shifting Nicu's attention. They weren't here alone. Without stopping to think about what she was doing, Kayla took advantage of the distraction and shoved three of the mannequins toward the center of the room where Nicu stood. A domino effect ensued as one by one the mannequins tumbled on top of one another across the room. Nicu took a step back as one of them crashed next to him.

Levi grabbed Kayla's hand and pulled her toward the door behind them.

"Stop! Both of you!"

A bullet hit one of the still standing mannequins. Its head exploded as they ducked into the next room. Any lingering doubts about Nicu's intentions had vanished. His solution was to ensure they were the next victims lying on a slab at the morgue.

She rounded the corner too quickly and a metal pole sticking out from the wall cut her calf, but adrenaline kept her from feeling more than a sting. Newspapers covered the front windows, blocking most of the sunlight. But at least they'd found their way out. A second shot ricocheted off the wall beside them.

More voices shouted from inside the warehouse, but she and Levi ignored them as they slipped out the front door and kept running. Kayla scanned the busy street, trying to orient herself as to where they were. If she was right, the tram shouldn't be more than four or five blocks east of them.

"We need to put as much distance between us and them as possible," Levi said. "How far to the nearest tram?"

"Not far if we hurry."

Kayla glanced behind her. There was no sign of Nicu, but that didn't mean he wasn't behind them, somewhere in the crowd.

She heard the warning bell of the tram that was pulling up as they approached the stop a couple minutes later. They jumped on board, where Levi paid his fare while she scanned her pass, then they hurried to two empty seats at the back.

"Do you still think we should go to the houseboat?" Kayla asked, sitting down next to the window as the tram continued down the track. She hadn't seen Nicu, but she wasn't convinced he wasn't still out there following them.

"Yes, I do."

"But if that's where Dad is, don't you think Nicu will head there as well?" she asked.

"Maybe, but that means we need to get there first." He sat down next to her. "Your leg's bleeding."

"It's nothing." She pulled a tissue from her bag, then wiped the blood off the cut, ignoring the sting.

"People are going to wonder what happened to us." She let out a low laugh, though her hands were still shaking. "Between your black eye, the goose egg on my head, the cut on your arm and now this we make quite a pair."

But any feelings of amusement quickly faded. She glanced out the window as bikes, pedestrians and buildings blurred past, with memories taking their place. Lilly's death. Her father's disappearance, Mercy running for her life, Nicu running after them…

How had this happened?

"What are you thinking?" he asked.

"So much about this situation brings up a slew of memories I'd rather lay to rest."

The uncertainty she'd felt after Lilly vanished. The horror of finding out what had happened to her. How throughout the entire situation she'd felt completely out of control. Like nothing she did or said could change what was happening around her.

She felt her heart tremor as he squeezed her

hand. Since when did he make her heart race like she was eighteen again? But no matter how hard she tried to fight the unexpected feelings she had for him, she couldn't get rid of them. Not completely.

"I'm so sorry," he said.

She shoved away the questions and shifted her thoughts back to Lilly.

"My sister is why I'm here and why I get up every morning. Losing her changed me," she continued. "You remember Lilly. For as long as I remember, she was the one with a hairbrush in her hand as a microphone performing for anyone who would listen. She dreamed of growing up and becoming the next big singing star or cover model. Anything as long as it was in the spotlight."

It had always seemed so innocent until someone took advantage of her and with it her life.

"I remember hearing about the issue of child trafficking back then," she continued, "but it wasn't a problem in small-town USA. It was something horrible that happened, but always to girls living in another country, far away from our idealistic life. But I was wrong. It doesn't matter what your race or skin color is as long as you are a girl who will listen to the lies and the promises. And that's what Lilly did."

Kayla watched a row of small boats bobbing in the water. "I still see Lilly as the little girl standing in front of the fireplace and singing her heart out. Not being raped a dozen times a day by men who paid to sleep with her."

"I'm so, so sorry that Lilly and your family had to go through all of this. Slavery should have been abolished centuries ago. To see it firsthand like this is sickening."

She looked up to him and caught his gaze. "I can't let them get Mercy, Levi. She's always reminded me of Lilly with her charismatic personality. They couldn't break Mercy's spirit. Not completely. But if Nicu finds her again…"

"Then we have to do everything in our power to make sure that doesn't happen."

"Thank you."

"For what?"

"For being here, so I don't have to face this alone."

Levi heard the pain in her voice, but there was something more than that—he also heard her determination. He'd seen firsthand how she'd taken a tragedy and turned it into a way to help other girls so they didn't end up like her sister. And yet he was certain even that knowledge didn't always help erase the pain she still harbored.

"I'm glad I'm here as well," he said. "Not because of what's happening, of course, but because you shouldn't have to go through this by yourself."

The last twenty-four hours had pushed both of them to the limits, and unfortunately it wasn't over yet. But suddenly—for one brief moment—everything that had happened managed to slip away, until all he could see was the woman sitting next to him.

"Do you remember that time I gave you a ride into town?" he asked, realizing the risk he was taking in changing the topic.

She let out a soft laugh. "How could I forget? I was on my way to a job interview. It was pouring down rain and I got a flat tire. You stopped to pick me up in your father's BMW. You have no idea how stressed I was getting into that car and knowing what a dripping mess I was. And knowing what your father would say—"

"I have a confession," he said. "I almost asked you out that day."

She glanced up at him, her eyes wide with surprise. "Really?"

He nodded, wondering what would have happened if he'd actually gone through with his plan. He hadn't told anyone, but he'd been thinking about it for weeks. Having her in the car with him had cemented the idea, but for some reason, in the end he'd chickened out.

"Why didn't you?" she asked.

"I decided you'd probably say no."

"You were wrong. I would have said yes," she said, her grin widening. "And since we're confessing, when Adam asked me out the first time, I said yes to him for all the wrong reasons."

"And what reason would that be?" he asked.

She ducked her head slightly. "I was…hoping you might get jealous and ask me out."

How had he missed that? There'd always been something about Kayla that had made him want to get to know her better. Something that had in turn managed to tangle up his tongue whenever he was around her.

Her freckled cheeks reddened slightly. "Makes me wonder what might have happened if you'd asked me out."

"Me, too, though apparently I was young and stupid."

"Hardly. I always looked up to you. You were the one who had it together. Then you went off and joined the military and I didn't think I'd ever see you again."

"And Adam kept asking you out."

How could he have been so stupid? But now...was he somehow being given a second chance?

"I should have asked you out."

"Except I know your father. He would never have let you go out with me."

"Why do you say that?"

"He was grooming you for the role of CEO of his company your entire life. Adam told me that you were supposed to go off to college, then take over the company. Which was why he totally flipped out when you joined the military."

"I know he did, but that didn't stop me. Just like I wouldn't let my father dictate who I date."

"Maybe, but I remember hearing grumblings at the plant. Your father wasn't always the easiest boss to work for. And I have a feeling it wasn't always easy to be his son, either." She pressed her lips together. "I'm sorry. I shouldn't have said that."

"No. You're right. And yet in the end, he still got his way. I'm back in Potterville heading up the family business. But maybe that is a good thing."

All the feelings he'd ever had toward her rushed through him. Before he could think about what he was doing, he leaned down and brushed his lips against hers. His heart pounded at her nearness as she pressed her hand against his chest and kissed him back. For a few brief seconds there were no concerns or worries about someone trying to kill them. Because right now, none of that mattered.

The loudspeaker announced another stop.

She pulled away from him and shook her head. "I'm sorry, Levi, but I can't do this."

"Kayla, I—"

"We need to get off." She stood up as the tram slowed to a stop.

He glanced up at her. Worry lines had settled across her forehead. Had he totally misread her? He followed her off the tram and toward the canal, regretting what he'd just done.

How had he been such a fool?

Three blocks away, they found the houseboat bobbing gently in the canal. He glanced around them, trying to focus. Trying to forget what it had felt like to kiss her. Despite the extra precautions he'd taken to ensure they hadn't been followed, he knew he couldn't be sure. Which had him worried.

He studied the nondescript boat that was painted a light tan with wooden trim around the windows. A couple chairs sat on a small deck next to several neglected potted plants. It looked as if no one had been here for quite a while.

"Are you sure this is the right house?" she asked.

"It seems to be the correct address."

Whether her father was onboard, though, was an entirely different question.

"A place like this is actually prime real estate," she said, standing beside him. "Permits to moor a home—especially in certain locations—can raise the value of the houseboat substantially. Though apparently I'm not the only person in the city lacking a green thumb."

There were no signs of anyone on board, but that didn't mean they hadn't left Kayla's father here.

"If he's here, he's somewhere inside," Levi said.

He glanced around. The last thing he wanted to do was get arrested for trespassing. But that seemed like the least of their worries at the moment. While Kayla walked in the opposite direction, Levi stepped onto the boat and started walking around the deck, trying to see if he could see inside. But each of the windows was covered by dark gray blinds.

"Levi?"

"There's no way to see inside," he said, stepping back onto the dock where she stood.

"I found an unlocked window," Kayla said.

He hesitated before following her, praying they didn't attract any attention with their search. But if it meant finding Max, he wasn't sure they had a choice. He slid open the window, then stepped into the houseboat. Inside, the cabin was small but efficient, and it only took a few seconds to search the entire space.

He stepped back into the center of the room and shook his head.

Another dead end. There was no one on the boat. If her father had been here, he was gone.

SIXTEEN

Kayla glanced around the cabin of the house-boat, desperate to find a clue—anything—that would tell them her father had been here. But instead there was nothing. And nowhere left to search.

"Levi...where is my father? He should be here. The bells in the video, the rental agreement you found—everything pointed to him being here."

She turned around and caught Levi's gaze, trying to ignore the turmoil raging inside her. She'd been so convinced they would find her father and this nightmare would be over.

But it wasn't.

She started opening up the drawers of a wooden desk that sat against the wall while avoiding his mesmerizing blue eyes staring back at her. Their unexpected kiss on the tram had thrown her, leaving her feeling off balance on a day that already had her reeling.

She was going to have to sort out whatever was happening between her and Levi later. For now, they needed to find her father.

"There has to be something here," she said. "Some kind of clue telling us what they've done with him."

"Kayla, we need to get out of here. If Nicu followed us—"

"Wait a minute…" Kayla pulled a large zippered pouch out of the back of one of the drawers. "These are passports."

"Passports?" he asked.

A sick realization washed through her as she started spreading them out across the table one by one. Each passport represented a girl who'd had her entire life ripped away.

"Nigerian. Romanian. Slovakian. Ukrainian. When they bring the girls into the country, they take their passports and any legal identification away."

"Why?"

"So they have nowhere to go. They're told they're now in the country illegally, and if they're caught, the authorities will send them to prison."

"But that's not true."

"No, but most have come from countries where things like that do happen. Corrupt officials make you have to guess at who's the good guy. Which to them isn't a chance worth taking."

Kayla flipped open one passport that belonged to a young girl from Slovakia. According to her date of birth, she was sixteen years old. She looked barely thirteen. "So they have no one to trust and are forced to do as they're told. They're usually told they need to work in order to pay back the price of the plane ticket and any other expenses."

"Which could take years, I'm assuming."

"Exactly."

Levi walked over to where she stood. "But I'm still trying figure out why they don't just run away. Maybe not to the police, but to someone else, even a client, for that matter. Surely someone would try to help them."

"You didn't see see Mercy's tattoo. The one reminding her of who she belongs to. These girls are completely controlled by fear. Even those who end up coming to us are terrified. Most came to support their family. They think they're coming to wait tables or work in a hotel. Some are sold and even resold, told they have to work to pay off the debt. Their phones are monitored and they have no internet access. If they protest, they are beaten or told their families back home will be killed."

A car backfired, and Kayla jumped.

"We need to go," Levi said, glancing toward the window. "If Nicu realizes we might have come here, he won't be far behind."

If he didn't already know where they were, Kayla thought. Somehow he always managed to find them. But not this time. She crawled back through the window behind Levi, then hurried off the boat and onto the street that ran along the canal, hoping no one had seen them.

"So where do we go now?" she asked, hurrying to keep up with his long stride.

"Somewhere where we can regroup and figure out what we're missing. We've narrowed it down to this area of the city. We have the passports now, which are proof of what he's doing. We've just got to narrow it down further. Another piece of property. Another address in the files. I had to have missed something in there."

"There's a café not far from here that should give us some privacy."

And that would also have enough people coming through to make her feel safer. They also still had the file she'd brought with her on Mercy, as well as the files they'd grabbed at the house where Nicu had held them. Maybe if they went over them again, they'd find something.

The bells of Westerkerk began their prelude in the background as they headed up the canal. She glanced at her watch. It was almost four o'clock, and they still had no idea where her father was. No idea what their next move should be.

God's pretty good at using ordinary—and even sometimes inadequate—people.

Levi's words replayed through her mind. It was what she wanted. To fight for what was right. For justice and truth. And she'd been willing to risk everything to save the girls they worked with.

But I don't know how to fight this anymore, God. I don't even know if it's possible to end this.

They started across one of the hundreds of bridges in the city as the bells continued to chime. The famous Amsterdam church with its striking blue crown on top of the steeple loomed ahead of them. Rembrandt had been buried as a poor man on the church grounds in the 1600s, and years later a memorial statue of Anne Frank had been added.

"Anne Frank, whose family was hidden from Nazi persecution during World War II, could hear the chimes from the attics where they hid," she said, filling the silence that had settled between them. "The tower clock was one of the few things she could see from the attic."

Corrie ten Boom. Anne Frank. Mercy. They'd all been affected by man's hatred and greed. Stolen lives. Shattered pieces that were sometimes impossible to put back together.

The church bells started chiming the hour. One. Two. Three. Four.

Four chimes.

Four o'clock.

Kayla paused. They *had* missed something.

"Levi...we need to recheck the video of my father." She turned to him in the middle of the bridge, shivering at the chill rising off the water as she tried to put together the pieces.

"Why?"

The bells stopped ringing.

"My father was taken sometime between one and three yesterday afternoon. I know that because I spoke with him just after lunch, and he was fine. When I got home, he was gone."

"Okay."

"The chimes play a short tune every fifteen minutes, twenty-four hours a day," she continued. "On the hour, there's more of a preamble like we just heard that's followed by chimes that ring equal to whatever hour it is."

"How many chimes were on that video?" he asked.

She pulled out her phone and replayed the video, this time counting the chimes. "Seven chimes. And yet when we received the video, it wasn't that late yet."

"This video was doctored." Levi took a step back from her. "They added the chimes to the soundtrack before sending it."

"But why?" she asked. "Why go to all of that trouble?"

"The only thing that makes sense is to try to throw us off in case we tried to narrow it down to this area—or if we went to the authorities."

"Which is exactly what happened. Nicu wanted us to assume your father was somewhere here. That's why he wasn't on the boat. He was probably never on the boat."

Levi pushed Play again. Kayla looked away from the screen. Watching her father stare into the camera and plead made her sick to her stomach.

"Did you catch something else?" she asked.

"Maybe." He played it again. "Listen to the background noise."

She watched once more.

"Did you hear that?" he asked.

A heavy weight pressed against her chest.

How had they missed the discrepancies in the video? Their failing to figure this out could cost her father his life.

"There are multiple dogs barking in the background."

"And they sound like the German shepherds we ran into."

"My father has to be there. At the house. But we never found signs of anyone else there."

"We could have missed something. An attic or basement, maybe a storage building on the property," he said. "Nicu followed us into town, but now that he's lost us, I'm going to guess that he's going to go back to the house and cut his losses."

"He knows that we'll come back and probably bring the authorities with us."

"Exactly. We didn't have time to search the entire property, which means if there are girls there, he's going to need to clear out any evidence."

"And my father? What about him? If Nicu cuts his losses…"

She couldn't finish her sentence. She could still hear the desperation in her father's voice on the video and see the fear in his eyes. They had to find him.

"We can't do this on our own anymore."

Levi caught her gaze. "Nicu's not playing by his own rules, and plus, I think we've finally got enough evidence of what he's doing to bring in the authorities."

She nodded, knowing he was right this time. Because not only was Nicu playing for keeps, he was willing to take down anyone who got in his way.

"You need to call your contact with the police department," Levi said, squeezing her fingers.

She pulled out her phone and quickly searched for his number in her contacts. "There was a law put into place a couple of years ago. If the inhabitants of a house are suspected of having illegal immigrants on their property, the police have the right to search without a warrant."

Her contact, Commissioner Bram Peeters, answered on the fourth ring.

"Commissioner Peeters? This is Kayla Brooks from International Freedom Operation."

"Kayla. It's good to hear from you." There was a slight pause on the line. "Is everything all right?"

"No, actually. I need your help regarding the kidnapping of an American citizen as well as a possible location being used by a group of human traffickers currently working here in Amsterdam."

"Who's been kidnapped?" he asked.

"My father." Kayla swallowed the lump in her throat, then proceeded to answer his string of questions, including the location of the estate.

"We can meet the authorities there," she said to Levi as she hung up the phone, weighing their options. "We could try to flag down a taxi, but Evi's not far from here, and she has a car we could borrow. I'd like to avoid getting any more civilians involved."

"Sounds like the best option we have."

She quickly dialed Evi's number, then waited for her to pick up. "If you're up to driving, I can navigate."

Levi felt the tension gripping his neck and shoulders as he sped down the long stretch of road in Evi's car toward the house where they'd been held hostage less than twelve hours ago. While he had no regrets getting the police involved at this point, the entire situation still left Levi with an uneasy feeling. Once again they had nothing concrete to assure them that Nicu had taken Max to the house. And even if he was there, they had no idea what they'd done to him, or even if he was still alive.

But while Levi's gut told him that they were on the right track, he hadn't missed the desperation in Kayla's eyes. She'd already lost both her sister and her mom. To lose her father this way would be devastating. All he could do now was pray they got to the house in time to find her father and have Nicu and his brother arrested. Then all of this would finally be over.

"We should be there in another couple minutes," she said, glancing at the GPS on her phone. "The driveway's just up the road."

He reached out and squeezed her hand, knowing how anxious she was. Her father's life was at stake here, and every second they didn't find him meant another second for Nicu to do the unthinkable.

A black sedan passed them, speeding in the opposite direction. Levi glanced in the rearview mirror.

It was Nicu.

"Hold on," Levi said. "That's them."

Levi pressed on the brakes, then quickly did a U-turn.

"Call Peeters and tell him we found Nicu and his brother," he said as they followed the sedan. "Tell them where we are and to get here as soon as possible."

"And if we catch up with them," she asked, turing on her phone. "What's your plan then?"

"I'm still working on that."

Because all he did know was if they lost them now, they could not only lose evidence of what Nicu was involved in, but there was a good chance that Kayla's father was in the back of the car. Which meant the only real option was to stop them now.

Levi sped up to the sedan on the narrow road, thankful there was no other traffic or bikes on the stretch of road at the moment.

"The authorities must have just missed them. The commissioner's on his way from the house right now," she said, hanging up the call. "But he told me he doesn't want us to get involved."

"That's funny." Levi frowned. "I'm pretty sure we already are involved."

Instead, the question should be how to stop the other vehicle without anyone—especially any passengers in the car—getting hurt. There was only one viable solution he knew of.

"Hang on, Kayla," he said, accelerating until he was alongside Nicu's vehicle. Gripping the steering wheel, he steered the front bumper of their car into the other vehicle, right behind the back tire. If the procedure worked, the move would send the car into a spin, which in turn should cause the engine to stall. A second later, Nicu's car lost traction and began skidding down the road, while Levi worked to stay clear of the vehicle. The other vehicle spun as predicted, then stalled out on the side of the road. Levi pulled to a stop in front of the sedan, blocking the road.

"You okay?" Levi turned to Kayla as he yanked off his seat belt and unlocked his door.

"I think so." Kayla pressed her hand against her chest. "Guess you learned more than just picking locks in the army."

"Yes, but two wrecked cars in one day would have my instructor's head spinning," he said, jumping out of the car. "Stay here. I'll be back."

"Levi—"

But he was already headed toward the other vehicle. The dust had yet to settle as he ran to the driver's side, where he was counting on Nicu to be disoriented from the maneuver. And while his plan was risky, he was out of options.

The driver's door opened as Nicu attempted to get out, but Levi quickly slammed it shut, managing to knock Nicu's gun out of his hand at the same time. The weapon skidded across the pavement. Levi quickly took a step back and grabbed the weapon.

"Get out, Nicu," he said, pulling open the driver's door. But this time he was armed.

He glanced into the car, still unable to see clearly into the back seat, but the passenger seat was empty.

"Where's your brother?" Levi asked.

"I don't know." Nicu touched his forehead and groaned.

"Get away from the car," someone shouted from behind him. "Both of you."

Levi turned around. Nicu's brother. Andrei held Kayla in front of him with his gun pressed to her temple, blocking any possible shot.

"I'm sorry, Levi," she said. "He grabbed me out of the car."

He frowned, but there was no time to spend regretting the fact that he'd missed this scenario.

"What are you doing, Andrei?" Nicu asked.

"Putting an end to all of this. You just couldn't leave things alone and walk away, could you, big brother?"

"What are you talking about? We're in this together. We've always been in this together."

"No…this is your mess, and I'm not going to let you take me down. Not this time."

"Andrei—"

"Enough! Get out of the car."

Sirens blared in the distance.

"Let her go," Levi said. "You're only going to make things worse for yourself."

"Like things could actually get any worse?" Andrei said. "Because here's what's going to happen. She's going with me. I'm going to get back into the car and no one is going to follow me, including you, Nicu. You're so obsessed with finding that girl that you don't know what you're doing anymore."

"You know I have to find her."

"You're a fool, Nicu. Mercy's gone. It's over. But I'm not going to throw my life away because of you."

"It's not over. She'll come back to me."

Levi took a step forward and aimed the confiscated gun at Andrei. "Put your gun down. It's over."

He wasn't going to lose Kayla again no matter what it took this time. Because he knew if she ended up getting into the car with Andrei, the odds were he'd never see her alive again.

Levi glanced to his right, where two police vehicles had just stopped.

"I want both of you to put your weapons down now," one of the officers shouted, pulling out his own gun.

Levi glanced at Kayla, then slowly set his weapon on the ground.

The cop turned to Andrei. "And you…step away from her now."

Andrei hesitated, then dropped his gun onto the ground beside him before holding his hands up. The commissioner signaled to his officers to handcuff the men.

"Commissioner," Kayla said, stepping forward, "this is Levi Cummings, former US Army counterintelligence."

"Nice to meet you," he said, shaking Levi's hand.

"It's nice to meet you as well, sir."

"That was quite a stunt you just pulled now, but it worked, even though I think I remember saying don't get involved."

"They would have gotten away, sir."

"Which is why we owe you a bit of gratitude. Turns out we have a thick file on Nicu and Andrei Dragan." He turned back to Kayla. "Are you okay?"

"I am now. He would have killed me if I'd left with him," she said. "But we need to check the back of the car, sir. We believe he might have some of the girls with him, or even my father."

One of the officers moved to search the car. "You're right. There are two girls here."

Kayla hurried over to them, pulled off her coat and wrapped it around one of the girls. "*Je nu veilig bent.* You're safe now."

She signaled for one of the officers to find a blanket for the other girl. "What about the trunk? We have to find my father."

"I just looked. I'm sorry, ma'am, but there's no one else in the car."

SEVENTEEN

Kayla watched the police lead Nicu and his brother toward the squad car. Hopefully now Mercy would never have to worry about them again. She was finally free from the man who had tormented her not just physically, but emotionally as well. And while IFO's program would ensure she continued to receive both the counseling and job training that she needed, Kayla also hoped that one day soon Mercy would be able to go back to Nigeria to see her family.

But where was her father?

Nicu's cold gaze pierced right through her as he walked past.

"Tell me where my father is," she said, catching up to him. "What did you do with him?"

Nicu shot her a smile, then spit at her.

A chill swept through her as she took a step backward.

"Ignore him," the commissioner said. "We're still searching the property, but all we've found so far is the guard's dead body."

A sick feeling washed through her. If Nicu had no qualms killing a man who'd worked for him, he'd certainly have no problem killing her father.

"I need to go to the house and help look for him," she said, heading back toward Evi's car, thankful the damage was minimal.

"Kayla, wait," the commissioner said. "You need to leave the search to us. We will find him."

Kayla spun around to face him. "It's my father, Commissioner. I need to help."

"I'm guessing you could use a couple extra people to help search the property," Levi added, pulling the car keys out of his pocket.

"Fine." The commissioner nodded, then started for his own car. "We'll meet you there."

The dogs were barking ferociously when they pulled through the open gate and up the long driveway of the house. Someone—presumably one of the officers—had tied the animals up outside the three-car garage, and they clearly weren't happy.

"Do you think they just planned to leave the dogs here?"

"I think all Nicu was worried about was getting those girls out of here before the police showed up. He was probably planning to leave the country."

And her father…what had they done with him?

One of the officers ran up to the commissioner's car.

"Something's going on," Kayla said.

She opened her door as soon as Levi shifted the car into Park.

"What's going on?" Kayla asked, hurrying toward the officers.

"They found your father," the commissioner said, meeting them halfway across the drive. "They were keeping him in a small closet at the back of the house."

"Please…please tell me he's okay." If Nicu had hurt him…

"I'm sorry, but I don't know yet. Medics are here and are with him right now—"

"I need to see him." Kayla pushed past the man and started sprinting across the lawn.

As she approached the house, two medics were wheeling her father out the front door on a stretcher

If anything had happened to him…

He was on an IV, and wrapped up with a heavy blanket around his shoulders and another one across his legs. She still didn't know what he'd had to endure since yesterday, but at least he was alive.

"Daddy?"

The medic waved her back. "I'm sorry, ma'am, but—"

"It's my father. Please. I need to see him. Is he okay?"

"We need to take him in for observation, but it looks as if he's just dehydrated." The medic glanced at his patient. "I can give you a minute with him."

"Thank you."

The medic moved back as Kayla ran her fingers across her father's bruised face. "I'm so, so sorry."

"Don't be. They knocked me around a bit, but I'm going to be okay." He squeezed her hand. "Besides, I have a feeling I look far worse than I feel."

"I hope so, because I'm not sure I like the rainbow look you've got going for you across your cheek. It clashes with your plaid shirt." Kayla laughed then gathered her father up in a hug. "But all that matters now is that you're alive."

"And what about you?" Her father pulled back and caught her gaze. "What did they do to you, Kayla? You look like you've been through your own nightmare."

"It's a long story, but I'm okay now that I know you're okay. Besides, I had someone with me the whole time."

"Who's that?"

She looked up to where Levi stood at the edge of the grass, giving them their space. "You know Levi."

"Levi Cummings?" Her father glanced up, noticing him for the first time. "What's he doing here?"

"Like I said, it's a long story."

"One I'd like to hear. Though between you and me, he's the only person in his family besides his mother who seems to have his head on straight. Of course, I've also always heard that he's quite a ladies' man, or at least that's what the magazines claim."

"More than likely a bunch of rumors, but even if it is true, I'm also not one of those swooning girls who falls for every handsome man who comes to my rescue."

She glanced back at Levi. Except this time, she had.

"I'll admit, you could do worse," her father said.

"What's that supposed to mean?"

"I remember telling your mother once that you were marrying the wrong brother."

"The wrong brother?" She furrowed her brow and lowered her voice so Levi couldn't overhear their conversation. "You never told me that."

"Well, I am now."

"Forget about that." She tried to squeeze back the tears. "All this made me realize I don't tell you I love you enough. I thought I was going to lose you, Daddy—"

"But you didn't. What about you, though? What happened to your leg?" he asked. "I noticed it as you were walking over here. You've got quite a large cut."

She looked down at her ripped pant leg where the blood had seeped through her pants before drying into a crusty patch of brownish red.

"It's nothing."

"Nothing?" Her father nodded toward the paramedics. "You need to get it checked out."

"I will, as soon as they've taken care of you."

"Promise?" he asked.

"I promise."

"Everything's going to be okay," Max said, squeezing her hand. "Everything's finally going to be okay."

She moved aside as one of the medics checked his IV, then headed for the ambulance.

"Looks like he's going to be okay," the commissioner said, stepping up beside her.

Kayla wiped away a stray tear and nodded. "Thanks to you."

"I certainly can't take all the credit. While I'm anxious to get your official statements, I want you to know that the two of you saved a lot of lives today. Those girls, Mercy and now your father... And I plan to do everything in my power to ensure those men get locked up for the rest of their lives."

Levi knocked on Kayla's door at nine thirty the next morning with a bag of pastries from a bakery he'd found a block away from her apartment. He still found it hard to believe all that had happened since the first time he'd knocked on her door two days ago.

Once he'd given his statement to the police the night before it had been dark by the time he made it back to his hotel. But as exhausted as he'd been, he'd still found himself unable to sleep. He'd finally gone to sleep, then slept until eight. Something he never did.

And today he still had no idea what he was

going to do about Kayla. He wasn't sure his heart could handle simply walking away.

Kayla's father opened the door.

"Mr. Brooks," Levi said. "It's good to see you again. How are you feeling?"

"Much better than I was yesterday, thanks, but please, why don't you call me Max. Mr. Brooks seems too formal."

"All right." Levi shut the front door behind him, then followed Max into the small room that was neat and organized this time. Which didn't surprise him.

"Looks as if you come bearing gifts," Max said.

"Bagels, chocolate croissants and a couple fruit tarts." Levi set the bag on the kitchen table. "I figured everyone should find something they like."

"I think the biggest problem will be how to choose. Can I get you some coffee? Kayla's getting dressed and will be out soon."

"I'm still trying to wake up, so, yes, I'd love some." Levi pulled back one of the chairs and sat down. "How did you sleep?"

"I'm not sure exactly what the doctor gave me to take, but I slept like a rock."

"I'd say that after all that happened, you needed a good night's sleep."

Max set a cup of coffee on the table in front

of Levi, then started putting the pastries he'd brought on a plate.

"I owe you my life, Levi. Both you and my daughter."

Levi smiled. "I'm just thankful I could be here to help Kayla. This could have ended a whole lot worse."

"For all of us." Max's gaze shifted to the door to the bathroom before turning back to Levi. "I am still curious as to why you came to Amsterdam."

Levi grabbed one of the chocolate croissants and took a bite before answering. "Adam was released from prison last week. He'd made some threats toward Kayla, and I was worried about her."

"So you flew halfway around the world to make sure she was safe?"

"It seemed like the right thing to do at the time."

Max sat down in the chair across from him. "Kayla always looked up to you. It's kind of ironic that you would be the one to help save both her and me."

"Maybe, but your daughter's a strong woman. I have a feeling she would have found a way to save Mercy without me."

"But it's always easier when you've got someone else at your side." Max poured an inch of cream into his own coffee mug, then added a spoonful of sugar. "When Kayla's mom died, I didn't know how I was going to keep living. For months I haven't known how to simply get out of bed in the morning and make it through the day. I've felt so alone, and if it weren't for Kayla... I don't know where I'd be right now. But you want to know what's crazy?"

"What's that?" Levi asked.

"I figured out early on what that man Nicu was involved in. And while I sat in the closet waiting for him to kill me, I thought about those girls who've had everything ripped away from them. Thought about how much I really have."

"Those feelings are legitimate, but you need to remember that those girls' losses don't diminish your own. Bereavement can be one of the hardest things we as humans face. Add to that the guilt that often comes with it. You're human. It's okay to give yourself time to grieve and heal."

"Maybe. I guess in the end, I just want Kayla to be safe. And to find what Maggie and I had."

Levi took a sip of his coffee, not sure what the man was getting at.

"You're in love with my daughter, aren't you?" Max asked.

"With Kayla?"

He shot him a smile. "Who else do you think I'm talking about?"

Levi took another sip of his coffee, suddenly feeling uncomfortable. "Until this trip, I hadn't seen her for years. We hardly know each other anymore."

"Maybe, but while you might need to do a bit of catching up, it isn't hard for me to see how you feel."

Levi shifted in his seat, wishing Kayla would appear and put an end to this conversation. "I'm still not sure I understand, sir."

"Besides the fact that you flew all the way here to make sure she was okay, there's something about your demeanor that changes when you talk about her. I was in love once. That look is hard to miss."

"She's just a friend, sir. Nothing more. And besides…things would never work out between us even if I did feel something toward her."

"Why? Because of your brother?"

"Yes."

"You want to know what I think?"

Levi nodded even though he was pretty sure Max was going to tell him anyway.

"Even if your brother hadn't gone to prison, I don't think things would have worked between them. She was always too good for him. She needs someone like you. Someone who's motivated, who's a leader and who is willing to put his life on the line for someone else. That's who she is. And from what I've always seen in you, that's who you are as well."

As much as he wanted to believe the older man, he'd seen Kayla's reaction on the tram when he'd kissed her. There was simply too much baggage between them. Adam. His own father. Not to mention a few thousand miles.

"Even if I did care about her," he said, "I'm not sure she sees it that way."

"You're as stubborn as your father, Levi Cummings. Maybe I'm wrong, but I'm pretty sure she feels the same way you do. Trust me. Give her some time. Maybe stick around a few days longer."

Levi's phone rang, pulling him away from the conversation. He glanced at the caller ID. Adam was calling.

"I'm sorry, but I need to take this call. It's my brother."

He stepped to the other side of the room, then answered the call.

"Levi, where are you? I've been trying to get a hold of you."

"I've been out of town the past few days," he said, grateful the police had found his phone while going through Nicu's house. "Where are you?"

"At a hotel in downtown Chicago."

"Chicago?" Levi caught his brother's slurred words. Was his brother drunk? "I thought you were going to Amsterdam to see Kayla."

"I was." There was a long pause on the line before he continued. "I wanted so much to get back at her. I'd even come up with half a dozen plans that would make her feel as miserable as I have the past two years. But in the end, I couldn't get on that plane. I was afraid I'd do or say something I'd regret. Instead I jumped in my car and started driving north."

"You sound drunk."

"I might have had a few drinks, but don't worry. I have no plans of doing anything stupid. I've learned my lesson."

He hoped so, but he wasn't convinced.

"Where are you?" Adam asked. "The connection's terrible."

"I'm in Amsterdam, actually."

"What? Have you seen Kayla?"

"I'm here with her now."

"Why in the world would you go to Holland to see Kayla?"

"I was worried about what you might do to her."

"So I say a bunch of stupid things, and you think you need to clean up another one of my messes."

"What did you expect me to do?"

Adam had ended up in prison, threatened Kayla... Was this how it was always going to be from now on? Him always trying to clean up the messes his brother had left behind?

"What happened to you, Adam? You had everything. A good job. An incredible fiancée...and you threw it all away for what?"

"We all know the answer to that one, now don't we?"

"Adam, I just want to help—"

"Leave me alone, Levi. I'm not even sure why I called. You've always been too self-righteous for my tastes."

Levi ignored the insult, shifting his attention instead to Kayla, who had just walked into the room.

"Listen, Adam..." Nothing he said was going to change for the moment. There were simply some things he couldn't fix. "We'll talk when I get back, but I've got to go for now."

She'd pulled her hair back in a ponytail and

was wearing an oversize sweater, jeans and a pair of boots. Max was right. He'd totally fallen for her. But that didn't mean she felt the same way, no matter what her father said. Still…maybe it wouldn't hurt if he stayed a few days longer.

"Hey," he said, shoving the phone into his pocket.

"Hey, yourself," she said. "You almost look like a new man."

"And you…you look rested."

And beautiful.

"Levi brought breakfast," Max said. "But I was thinking that the two of you should go out for a while. Get some fresh air." He grabbed one of the fruit tarts.

"I can't leave you here alone, Daddy."

"Why not? You've been hovering over me ever since we got back. The doctor says I'm fine, and besides that, I could really use some quiet."

"Daddy…are you sure you're okay?"

"Perfectly fine. And while you're out, would you mind picking up some of those Chinese spring roll things for lunch?"

"Loempia?" she asked.

"Yes."

"Well, at least you've got your appetite back," she said, kissing him on the forehead before turning to Levi. "What do you say? Are you up to giving my dad some space and going out for a while? It's cold, but I could use some fresh air."

He couldn't help but smile. "I think I can handle that."

And maybe in the process, he'd find the courage to tell her the truth about how he felt.

EIGHTEEN

Kayla glanced out over the popular Amsterdam canal, where rows of boats bobbed in the water. An unexpected cold front had hit the city last night, so those who dared go outside were bundled up in hats, scarves and gloves like she was. But she barely noticed the drop in temperature as she and Levi walked side by side past a familiar row of tall crooked houses springing up from the frozen mass of ground.

The terror of the last couple days might finally be over, but she was still trying to sort out her emotions. Nicu and his brother were in prison. Mercy and the other girls were safe. Her father was home. Everyone she cared for was okay. But if that was all true, then why did she feel so lost and confused?

She glanced at Levi's solid profile and felt her breath catch. There was no reason for him to stay in Amsterdam anymore and protect her. And as for the brief kiss they'd shared on the tram… She'd told herself to forget the way she felt when he'd kissed her. That it had been nothing more than an intense emotional reaction to what was going on around them. He didn't care for her. Not that way. And just because he'd managed to fill her dreams and her daydreams the past couple days didn't make that true.

"I spoke with Mercy this morning," she said, breaking the silence between them.

"How is she?"

"Still shaken up, but I was encouraged by some of the things she said. She's strong, and I really think she's going to be able to move forward, even after all that happened. And it helps knowing Nicu and his brother won't be able to hurt her again."

"I'm so glad to hear that," he said. "I still struggle imagining what those girls have gone through. Getting to the other side of the trauma can't be easy."

"It's not, but you understand that." She tightened the belt on her coat, wishing the weather was a few degrees warmer. "I also got a call from Beverly."

"Our Good Samaritan? Is she okay? I haven't stopped feeling guilty about leaving her. I even thought we needed to track her down."

"I thought the same thing, but this should make you feel better. She told me she was tired of card games, charity dinners and garden parties, and that meeting us was the most exciting thing that had happened to her in as long as she could remember."

Levi laughed. "You're kidding me."

"Nope. She also said not to worry about the car. The damage was minimal and worth every penny."

"That's definitely not what I expected to hear."

"Me, either, but I promised her I'd visit her in the next couple weeks."

"I have a feeling she'll thoroughly enjoy that."

"Me, too."

"Do you mind if I change the subject?" he asked.

"Of course not."

"I've been wanting to apologize," he said.

"Apologize?" His admission took her off guard. "For what?"

"On the tram when I kissed you… I never should have done that. Emotions were high, and I took advantage of the situation."

I took advantage of the situation.

She shoved her hands into her pockets. So that was it. He wasn't twenty anymore, and he hadn't kissed her because he had feelings for her. He'd kissed her because some madman had been chasing them, and in the process he'd gotten caught up in playing her hero.

Which was really the same reason she'd pushed him away. At that moment, dealing with her father's kidnapping and Mercy's disappearance had left her with zero energy to figure out what she felt toward him.

To admit to herself she was falling for him.

"Forget it," she said. "You don't owe me an apology."

"I just didn't want that hanging between us. Because I thought I might stay a few more days. That is, if you don't mind."

She looked up at him, surprised he'd have time to stay. "Of course not, but what about your job?"

"I am the CEO," he said. "And besides, the work will still be there when I get back. I heard you were taking a few days off, and I thought you might have time to give me a tour of the city."

"I think that could be arranged. What did you want to see?"

"My mother gave me a long list of things not to miss, but I'm thinking you already know the best places to visit."

She shoved aside any feelings of regret

along with any lingering emotion she felt toward him. There was no use wondering what could have happened between them.

"We could go ice-skating later," she threw out. "But there's also something else every tourist needs to experience."

"Besides being kidnapped?"

"Funny." She shot him a grin. "I was talking about eating herring."

"Herring? Wait a minute." He stopped in the middle of the walkway and faced her. "Can I be honest? That's the one thing I was hoping to avoid while I was here."

She couldn't help but laugh at his reaction. And after the stress of the past few days, it felt good to laugh. "I don't think I can let you get out of this. It's tradition, really."

"Tradition? I can think of a dozen other traditions I'd jump at participating in. Decorating the Christmas tree, sending flowers for Valentine's Day, carving the Thanksgiving turkey, but herring?"

"Trust me. People have been doing this for hundreds of years." She headed toward a street stand that sold the raw herring. "All you have to do is hold it by the tail, dip it into the raw onions and slide it into your mouth—"

"Raw onions?"

"Not up to the challenge?" she asked, wishing she didn't enjoy his flirting so much.

"Oh, I'm always up for a challenge." He stopped again, forcing her to turn back around. "But there is another reason to avoid herring and onions."

"And what would that be?"

He caught her gaze as she walked back toward him, making her heart tremble. "What if I wanted to kiss you again?"

She opened her mouth, then shut it. This time she had no idea how to respond. He'd already apologized. She'd understood it was because he'd regretted kissing her the first time.

So why did he want to kiss her again?

"I have a confession," he said. "Remember what I said to you on the tram about that day when I picked you up in the rain? How I thought about asking you out?"

She nodded. Her legs were shaking, but she wasn't sure if it was from the cold anymore, or from the way he was looking at her.

"I need to tell you the rest of the story."

She tugged on the end of her scarf. "Okay."

"Do you remember the day we trespassed on Mr. Sander's land and that bull…what was its name?"

"Agnes."

"Agnes. How could I forget? Anyway, I fell in love with you that day."

"What? I thought you hated me back then."

"I never hated you. You were wearing a pink-and-black T-shirt with butterflies and pink tennis shoes that day."

"I can't believe you remember something like that."

"I remember how pretty you were. How you always made me laugh. How you always had something nice to say to everyone."

"Why didn't you tell me years ago? Like that day you picked me up in the rain?"

Would things have turned out differently if she'd known how he felt?

"Like I told you before, I was never good at talking to girls back then. But now I've realized that I wasted half my life not stopping to listen to my heart. A part of me feels like this is a second chance. Because I almost lost you, Kayla. That night they grabbed us off the street…when I woke up and you were gone and I had no idea where you were, all I knew was that if they did anything to you, I don't know what I would have done."

She took a step closer to him, then rested her hands against his chest. "You're right. Raw onions aren't exactly conducive to a kiss. But another kiss wouldn't change anything."

"What do you mean?"

"You're leaving in a few days, and I'll still be here."

"What if I decided not to leave?"

She looked up at him, wanting to believe something could actually happen between them, but there were so many things standing in the way.

"I don't understand."

"Six months ago, I was offered a job. Working with both government and commercial customers on a consulting team for things like security management and techniques. They have a branch located in Europe that they are busy developing."

"And you could stay here? In Amsterdam?"

"I'd need to travel some, but most of the work could be done from wherever I'm living. I'd be doing a lot of the same things I did when I was in the army. Working to implement individual, specific plans for security requirements. I'd work with other instructors to train and consult these companies looking to bring their security up to the twenty-first century."

"It sounds perfect for you. But that would mean you'd leave your father's business."

"I never planned to stay. I'd need to make

sure the transition went smoothly, but my father doesn't need me. Not really. He has a dozen capable leaders in the company who are more than qualified to take the company to the next level. Kayla, I'm sorry if this is coming at you too fast. I guess I was hoping that you felt the same way, because I've realized it doesn't matter if I'm living in Potterville, Amsterdam or… Beijing, for that matter. There's only one person who I've ever imagined spending the rest of my life with. And that's you."

Her breath caught as she looked up at him and realized the truth. How had she missed it all these years?

She was in love with Levi Cummings.

"I don't want to walk away from the best thing to happen to me," he said. "Not again. I don't know what the future holds, but who does? What I do know is that I want to discover it with you."

"Stop," she said.

"Stop?"

"Trying to convince me." She wrapped her arms around his neck and smiled up at him. "What about that kiss?"

She forgot about the onions and the fish. Forgot about everything around her as he pulled her into his arms and pressed his lips against hers.

Because this time, she was going to follow her heart.

* * * * *

If you enjoyed this story by Lisa Harris,
pick up these previous titles:

TAKEN
DESPERATE ESCAPE
DESERT SECRETS
FATAL COVER-UP

Available now from
Love Inspired Suspense!

Find more great reads at
www.LoveInspired.com

Dear Reader,

I hope you enjoyed reading Kayla and Levi's story! Several years ago, my family and I visited friends in Holland on our way back to the US. One of the places we went to was the Corrie ten Boom museum in Haarlem. At one point, we actually stood in the narrow closet, the secret hiding place that was constructed for when the house was raided. I can't even imagine the fear those in hiding must have felt, knowing that men who wanted them dead were so close.

What I love about Kayla and Levi's story is the reminder of how God can use each one of us to make a difference in the lives of others. Most of us won't have to go through the things that they went through, but each one of us can impact those around us for good.

Be a blessing today!

Lisa Harris

Get 2 Free Books,

Plus 2 Free Gifts—
just for trying the
Reader Service!

YES! Please send me 2 FREE Love Inspired® Romance novels and my 2 FREE mystery gifts (gifts are worth about $10 retail). After receiving them, if I don't wish to receive any more books, I can return the shipping statement marked "cancel." If I don't cancel, I will receive 6 brand-new novels every month and be billed just $5.24 for the regular-print edition or $5.74 each for the larger-print edition in the U.S., or $5.74 each for the regular-print edition or $6.24 each for the larger-print edition in Canada. That's a saving of at least 13% off the cover price. It's quite a bargain! Shipping and handling is just 50¢ per book in the U.S. and 75¢ per book in Canada.* I understand that accepting the 2 free books and gifts places me under no obligation to buy anything. I can always return a shipment and cancel at any time. The free books and gifts are mine to keep no matter what I decide.

Please check one:

☐ Love Inspired Romance Regular-Print   ☐ Love Inspired Romance Larger-Print
    (105/305 IDN GMWU)   (122/322 IDN GMWU)

Name	(PLEASE PRINT)

Address		Apt. #

City	State/Province	Zip/Postal Code

Signature (if under 18, a parent or guardian must sign)

Mail to the **Reader Service:**
IN U.S.A.: P.O. Box 1341, Buffalo, NY 14240-8531
IN CANADA: P.O. Box 603, Fort Erie, Ontario L2A 5X3

Want to try two free books from another line?
Call 1-800-873-8635 today or visit www.ReaderService.com.

*Terms and prices subject to change without notice. Prices do not include applicable taxes. Sales tax applicable in N.Y. Canadian residents will be charged applicable taxes. Offer not valid in Quebec. This offer is limited to one order per household. Books received may not be as shown. Not valid for current subscribers to Love Inspired Romance books. All orders subject to approval. Credit or debit balances in a customer's account(s) may be offset by any other outstanding balance owed by or to the customer. Please allow 4 to 6 weeks for delivery. Offer available while quantities last.

Your Privacy—The Reader Service is committed to protecting your privacy. Our Privacy Policy is available online at www.ReaderService.com or upon request from the Reader Service.

We make a portion of our mailing list available to reputable third parties that offer products we believe may interest you. If you prefer that we not exchange your name with third parties, or if you wish to clarify or modify your communication preferences, please visit us at www.ReaderService.com/consumerschoice or write to us at Reader Service Preference Service, P.O. Box 9062, Buffalo, NY 14240-9062. Include your complete name and address.

LI17R3

Get 2 Free Books,
Plus 2 Free Gifts—
just for trying the
Reader Service!

YES! Please send me 2 FREE Harlequin® Heartwarming™ Larger-Print novels and my 2 FREE mystery gifts (gifts worth about $10 retail). After receiving them, if I don't wish to receive any more books, I can return the shipping statement marked "cancel." If I don't cancel, I will receive 4 brand-new larger-print novels every month and be billed just $5.49 per book in the U.S. or $6.24 per book in Canada. That's a savings of at least 19% off the cover price. It's quite a bargain! Shipping and handling is just 50¢ per book in the U.S. and 75¢ per book in Canada*. I understand that accepting the 2 free books and gifts places me under no obligation to buy anything. I can always return a shipment and cancel at any time. The free books and gifts are mine to keep no matter what I decide.

161/361 IDN GMWQ

Name	(PLEASE PRINT)

Address	Apt. #

City	State/Prov.	Zip/Postal Code

Signature (if under 18, a parent or guardian must sign)

Mail to the **Reader Service:**
IN U.S.A.: P.O. Box 1341, Buffalo, NY 14240-8531
IN CANADA: P.O. Box 603, Fort Erie, Ontario L2A 5X3

Want to try two free books from another line?
Call 1-800-873-8635 today or visit www.ReaderService.com.

*Terms and prices subject to change without notice. Prices do not include applicable taxes. Sales tax applicable in N.Y. Canadian residents will be charged applicable taxes. Offer not valid in Quebec. This offer is limited to one order per household. Books received may not be as shown. Not valid for current subscribers to Harlequin Heartwarming Larger-Print books. All orders subject to approval. Credit or debit balances in a customer's account(s) may be offset by any other outstanding balance owed by or to the customer. Please allow 4 to 6 weeks for delivery. Offer available while quantities last.

Your Privacy—The Reader Service is committed to protecting your privacy. Our Privacy Policy is available online at www.ReaderService.com or upon request from the Reader Service.

We make a portion of our mailing list available to reputable third parties that offer products we believe may interest you. If you prefer that we not exchange your name with third parties, or if you wish to clarify or modify your communication preferences, please visit us at www.ReaderService.com/consumerschoice or write to us at Reader Service Preference Service, P.O. Box 9062, Buffalo, NY 14240-9062. Include your complete name and address.

HOMETOWN HEARTS ♥

YES! Please send me **The Hometown Hearts Collection** in Larger Print. This collection begins with 3 FREE books and 2 FREE gifts in the first shipment. Along with my 3 free books, I'll also get the next 4 books from the Hometown Hearts Collection, in LARGER PRINT, which I may either return and owe nothing, or keep for the low price of $4.99 U.S./ $5.89 CDN each plus $2.99 for shipping and handling per shipment*. If I decide to continue, about once a month for 8 months I will get 6 or 7 more books, but will only need to pay for 4. That means 2 or 3 books in every shipment will be FREE! If I decide to keep the entire collection, I'll have paid for only 32 books because 19 books are FREE! I understand that accepting the 3 free books and gifts places me under no obligation to buy anything. I can always return a shipment and cancel at any time. My free books and gifts are mine to keep no matter what I decide.

262 HCN 3432 462 HCN 3432

Name   (PLEASE PRINT)

Address   Apt. #

City   State/Prov.   Zip/Postal Code

Signature (if under 18, a parent or guardian must sign)

Mail to the **Reader Service:**
IN U.S.A.: P.O. Box 1867, Buffalo, NY. 14240-1867
IN CANADA: P.O. Box 609, Fort Erie, Ontario L2A 5X3

* Terms and prices subject to change without notice. Prices do not include applicable taxes. Sales tax applicable in NY. Canadian residents will be charged applicable taxes. This offer is limited to one order per household. All orders subject to approval. Credit or debit balances in a customer's account(s) may be offset by any other outstanding balance owed by or to the customer. Please allow 4 to 6 weeks for delivery. Offer available while quantities last. Offer not available to Quebec residents.

Your Privacy—The Reader Service is committed to protecting your privacy. Our Privacy Policy is available online at www.ReaderService.com or upon request from the Reader Service.

We make a portion of our mailing list available to reputable third parties that offer products we believe may interest you. If you prefer that we not exchange your name with third parties, or if you wish to clarify or modify your communication preferences, please visit us at www.ReaderService.com/consumerschoice or write to us at Reader Service Preference Service, P.O. Box 9062, Buffalo, NY. 14240-9062. Include your complete name and address.

READERSERVICE.COM

Manage your account online!

- Review your order history
- Manage your payments
- Update your address

*We've designed the
Reader Service website
just for you.*

Enjoy all the features!

- Discover new series available to you, and read excerpts from any series.
- Respond to mailings and special monthly offers.
- Browse the Bonus Bucks catalog and online-only exculsives.
- Share your feedback.

Visit us at:
ReaderService.com